Finn's Going

TOM KELLY

Greenwillow Books

An Imprint of HarperCollins*Publishers*

I would like to add a special thanks to Anne for her tireless support of my book and to Virginia, my editor at Greenwillow, whose fresh insight helped push the book in a much, much richer direction.

Finn's Going

Copyright © 2007 by Tom Kelly

First published in 2007 in Great Britain by Macmillan Children's Books.

First published in 2007 in the United States by Greenwillow Books.

Epigraph from "The Waking," by Theodore Roethke. *Roethke: Collected Poems,* Doubleday Books.

The right of Tom Kelly to be identified as the author of this work has been asserted by him.

The text of this book is set in Granjon. Book design by Victoria Jamieson.

Library of Congress Cataloging-in-Publication Data

Kelly, Tom, (date).

Finn's going / by Tom Kelly.

p. cm.

"Greenwillow Books."

Summary: A ten-year-old boy decides to run away after the sadness at home becomes unbearable following the death of his twin brother.

ISBN: 978-0-06-121453-0 (trade bdg.) ISBN: 978-0-06-121454-7 (lib. bdg.)

[1. Death—Fiction. 2. Grief—Fiction. 3. Loss (Psychology)—Fiction. 4. Runaways—Fiction. 5. England—Fiction.] I. Title.

PZ7.K29855 Fi 2007 [Fic] 22 2006050121

First American Edition 10 9 8 7 6 5 4 3 2 1

 Greenwillow Books

Molly is brilliant (and Kitty is too).
Fionnuala Donnelly isn't too bad either.
And Sarah Manson, who really knows her onions.

I learn by going where I have to go.

—Roethke

Part One
Thinking

A brick with three holes in it (part one)

I didn't want to put a brick with three holes in it through Old Grundy's window. But I just couldn't think of any other way to get at that stupid stuffed otter of his.

I dug the brick out of the rockery in our back garden. That was on Saturday, the day after I started speaking again, when I finally told them my name. I hadn't said a thing for six weeks. Don't ask me why because I'm not really sure myself yet.

The rockery is my mum's idea of a joke. It's really a pile of rubble left over from the new shed. My dad reclaimed the bricks from a building site because reclaimed bricks are more environmentally friendly. Obviously not all three-holed bricks are reclaimed or better for the environment. I mean, there isn't any law about it. At least none *I've* heard of.

My dad spent the whole of last summer building the shaky shed. He uses it to keep *his* dad's carpentry tools in. He doesn't get to use them much because he spends most of his time teaching kids like me. It's one of the slightly smaller things that get him down. The news on TV is another. Sometimes he even shouts at the TV and calls politicians rude names.

My dad doesn't teach me because he said it would be unbearable for both of us. He's sad most of the time now since the thing with Finn. He doesn't speak very much either because he's too busy counting everything he can find to count, and speaking is one of the things my family doesn't really do anymore since Finn.

Putting a brick through Old Grundy's window makes me feel sad just telling you about it. Holt Street, where I live, isn't the kind of street that just leaves eco-friendly bricks lying around. I'm not saying we're poor. We just don't leave bricks lying around, either, if you know what I mean.

That's something you have to know about me from the start—I'm always going off on one. My mum says I'm highly imaginative but my dad says I suffer from acute diarrhea of the mouth. So you can take your pick. If you want to, you can skip those things when you feel like it.

A brick with three holes in it (part two)

When I finally dug the brick out I also didn't immediately think *This is exactly the right reclaimed brick to put through Old Grundy's front window.*

I'm not saying the plan wasn't sneaking around inside my head for a while because it was. But it wasn't an:

X = the front window

Y = the place by the hedge

Z = the brick with three holes soon to pass through X

kind of plan, either.

Though I did wash the mud and cat poo off the brick before I put it inside my schoolbag beside the maths homework I keep forgetting to do.

Sunday seemed to go on forever. It felt like it was made up of the time you get at the dentist's and I kept on thinking *Am I really going to do this? Am I really going to do this?* The next thing I knew it was Monday morning and I was running away from Briggs Street in case Old Grundy'd called the cops already.

Even though I'm on the run now and even though I'm not going to school, I have to stop at Clemens Road to do touch 1 touch 2 touch 3.

Clemens Road has a lot of trees still on it. It also has a lot of hedges that have been trimmed into animal shapes, like birds and cats and giraffes. It makes the street look like a zoo where all the animals have paused for a photograph while escaping. They're covered in car fumes but they still look alive. Touch 1 touch 2 touch 3 is this game I made up about a million years ago but I can't stop doing it no matter what. And it changes depending upon what's going on. It started off as just one of those things you do. But it stopped being a laugh and became more like work, like the time Finn and me cut Old Grundy's garden for him.

Now I just have to do it. I have to run up to the tree outside number 9[1] and touch it three times saying, "Touch 1 touch 2 touch 3." Next I have to do the tree at number 10[2] then I have to go back and do number 5[3]. Lastly I have to go back to number 10 again[4].

---

[1] When it happened to Finn
[2] My age at the moment
[3] My sister Angela's age at the moment
[4] Because I didn't have a real birthday this year

About Old Grundy

I know in things like this people like to know what other people look like and that sort of thing. So I'll put it in as I remember it.

Grundy is a graying crumple with no teeth who looks like he should be in a cartoon or something. His hands are amazing because they twist and turn like old tree roots and look too big for him. He also has the biggest ears I've ever seen. I asked my dad about this. He said men's ears keep on growing no matter what. He also said their noses keep on growing, too. For ages Finn and me followed all these old blokes around to see if my dad was winding us up or not.

Turns out it's true.

Another thing about Old Grundy is he was always cracking one off. And it wasn't just the noise, either. I mean, it isn't exactly whiz-popping or anything like that. This one time we were helping him cut his back garden. Finn and me were at the other end of the garden raking up the cut grass. It was hot but there was a breeze that kept blowing things toward us. Old Grundy just kept cracking them off one after another. And the breeze kept shoving the radiation cloud down toward our end of the garden. You could even smell them over the smell of cut grass. And that's quite a strong smell. The weird thing was that Old Grundy kept pretending that nothing was happening. No matter how loud or lethal, he just went on using his lawn mower. I couldn't look at Finn because he kept pretending to choke and his face always makes me want to laugh myself to bits anyway. Which is funny because it looks like mine.

One hundred and twelve upright vacuum cleaners and counting

Old Grundy's lived at number sixty-six since the beginning of time. He lives on his own with his amazing collections and he smells of fish and chips.

Old Grundy has two hundred and seventy-nine portraits of the queen hanging all over the walls of his spare room. I know because I looked one time. There were a lot but I can't say, "Yes, I counted them and there are exactly two hundred and seventy-nine of them." I didn't bother counting them because, well, that would be as mad as collecting them in the first place.

One time I asked Old Grundy why two hundred and seventy-nine and not two hundred and eighty or a googolplex or something. Old Grundy said, "One hundred and twelve upright vacuum cleaners and counting." This must've made some sense to him because it didn't make any to me at all.

His most worrying collection, though, is three hundred and fourteen stuffed animals.

◎

12 stuffed badgers

27 stuffed cats

3 stuffed snakes

12 of his stuffed pet dogs [2]

2 1/2 stuffed crocodiles

39 stuffed owls

1 stuffed otter [3]

12 stuffed eagles

9 stuffed robins

4 stuffed gerbils

653 stuffed mice

1 stuffed laughing hyena [4]

2 very stuffed lions

[1] I know there were more but I can't remember them all.
[2] Sometimes Donut looks stuffed.
[3] Now flattened by my eco-friendly brick
[4] Not laughing anymore

The groove my feet have worn

I try to walk normally even though I'm really running away and my belly's gurgling like that time Finn had that sore throat. I go toward the bus stop even though I know I'm not going to school, even though I probably won't ever go to school ever again. Truth is I don't even know why I'm doing this. The trouble is everything still looks so normal but it doesn't feel normal. All the houses and the gardens and cars are doing all the things they always do. But they just feel different.

It's like my feet think this is what always happens so it always will. It's like they've worn a groove or something. I may be just a kid, but I know things never stay the same. No matter what.

Even though all the houses and gardens and cars will look the same tomorrow, they won't be. Even though the bus stop will still be there tomorrow and tomorrow and tomorrow, things won't be the same. If you look you can see things changing every single second of the day and night. Things get broken, things get fixed, things get lost, and things get found. Or sometimes they just stay broken or lost.

All this stuff sneaks up on you so it's hard to spot. And there's nothing you can do about it. It's just the way things are.

As I walk toward the bus stop I'm trying hard not to feel sorry for my stupid feet. I know that sounds mad but you have to be careful about these things. There's just too many things to feel sorry for. My mum says that's what's wrong with my dad.

Things my dad feels sorry for:

People who get hurt

People who are hungry

People who give up[1]

People who are lost

People who are afraid all the time

People who are rubbish at DIY[2]

People who are forced to do things they don't
   want to do

People who think they need guns

People who are going bald

People who don't feel sorry for anyone

[1] I don't know what that means.
[2] Do It Yourself

Beast + wooden fence + rusty razor wire + tin foil and garbage bin liners=

There's this terrible beast dog living at number forty-two on the corner of Ahlberg Row. All the local kids are scared of it because no one's ever seen it. The beast lives behind one of those high wooden fences you can't see through. If it got out you just know it would rip you to pieces in about two seconds flat. And it's always trying to get out. It's always throwing itself at the fence and making it shudder like mad. Bobby Thompson said he heard it did escape once and it bit some kid's willy right off. I don't think that's true for several reasons. The first is Bobby Thompson is a big fat liar. The second is it would have had to help him get his trousers off or the kid mustn't have been wearing any. And who'd be mad enough to do that? Even Airplane Kev wouldn't be that mad.

It's called the beast because no one knows what its real name is or even what it looks like. And even if you wanted to climb up the fence, say on someone's shoulders, so you could look over and see what it's like, you can't. You can just forget it because of the big scrolls of rusty razor wire wound along the top. Razor wire catches you and slices you up. So you'd have to be left there because if anyone else tried to help you, they'd get caught too. The rust would give you blood poisoning and you'd die anyway. It would just be slower and hurt more.

No one knows who even owns the beast. The upstairs windows you can just see through the razor wire have tin foil and black garbage bin liners taped all over them. I suppose that's in case you have binoculars or a telescope or something else for seeing things up close that are far away. I think that's a bit mad. Because you wouldn't even know when to get up or go to bed or anything like that. When I mentioned it to my dad he said they would know because at night there wouldn't be any kids around to make the beast throw itself at the fence and make it shudder and make the razor wire sing. He also said:

"Beast + wooden fence + rusty razor wire + tin foil and black garbage bin liners = definitely not wanting to be bothered by anyone ever."

So I said:

"Beast + wooden fence + rusty razor wire + tin foil and black garbage bin liners = definitely people always turning up to bother you."

Even though I disagreed with him he grinned because he's a physics teacher and he's always encouraging me to do maths even though I hate it. He always says, "Maths can be fun if you let it." This is one of the things he says that I definitely don't believe.

Bod and Airplane Kev

As I turn the corner of Clemens Road the barking gets louder and madder. I can also hear the razor wire singing. I spot two other uniforms at the shuddering fence. I'm still wearing mine but I have some of my own clothes to change into at the toilets at the bus station.

It's Airplane Kev and Bod, who're both in my year at school. Usually I don't go near them because they're too mad. They're not evil or anything. I'm not saying that. They're just mad. But considering what I've done, I suppose that makes me pretty mad too.

When I get closer, Bod nods without saying anything. No one knows why he's called Bod. He just is. Bod has flat eyes and a flat expression. One side of his face is crumpled like a drink tin from where part of a house fell on him one time. He's hard to understand when he *does* say something. The only person who understands him is Airplane Kev.

Airplane Kev is called Airplane Kev because he's always going on about airplanes. He gets so excited he makes a spluttering sound like an old airplane. And he only ever gets really excited when he's talking about airplanes. So, unlike with Bod, you don't have to be a genius to work out why he's called Airplane Kev.

If you ever meet him, don't mention jets of any description unless it's to say they're rubbish. Airplane Kev really hates jets, any kind of jet. He once had a fight with someone because they said jets were better than biplanes.

Another thing about Airplane Kev is his bigness. Even if you're really big yourself, you feel very small beside him. He's big the way an elephant is big. He looks like some skinny kid who's been inflated with a bicycle pump after he's been put in his clothes. Some people call him Inflatable Kev but never to his face. His face is the smallest thing about him. He has tiny little eyes that stare so much your own eyes feel sorry for them and start stunt-watering instead.

Airplane Kev says, "Danny or Finn?" He says it before he realizes because everyone always says it. Then when he does realize because Bod kicks him on the leg, he gets this terrible sick look on his tiny face. I feel instantly sorry for him. I feel sorry for him because I don't really know how to do anything else at the moment.

I feel sorry for everybody.

Poor Airplane Kev kicks the fence as hard as he can to get past saying it. I know he has hurt his foot, so I say, "Danny" in a normal voice to make him feel better. I say it quietly but they still wouldn't have heard if I'd shouted it as loud as I can.

The Beast chooses this moment to fling itself at the fence. That's another weird thing about it. The Beast will always match how hard you shake the fence.

The whole fence starts shaking and shuddering and the rusty razor wire starts singing its head off. We all jump at exactly the same time. And I think, *Here comes the Beast, here comes the Beast*, and, *Maybe he really did bite that kid's willy off for him*.

I look at Airplane Kev and Bod and they look at me. Then we start laughing. Bod says, "Ten p, five p."

And this makes us laugh even more because that's exactly what happens.[1] Then Bod does his hiss-hiss and hiss punctured-tire laugh.

The Beast:

always makes you jump

always makes your bum go ten p/five p

even though you know it's going to happen

---

[1] If you don't know, ten p/five p is your bum going splutter-splutter when you're suddenly really scared.

even though you know your bum will go

ten p/five p

you just can't help it.

"Ten p/five p," says Airplane Kev. He's trying to keep the laugh going. Instead he just makes it go flat quicker.

Bod goes hiss-hiss and hiss again but this time it's at Airplane Kev for making it all go flat. And even though he's not the sharpest tool in the box, Airplane Kev knows.

But Airplane Kev is good at getting past things like this because he has to all the time. So he says, "Your turn, Danny." And not only does he say it, he says it like he's doing me the biggest favor in the whole world.

Bod just points his dry hiss-hiss and hiss at me as he steps back.

Cheers Airplane Kev.

So I drop my bag and walk over to the fence. I walk as if it's the most boring thing in the world even though my bottom's going ten p/five p. All the time the fence is shaking and shuddering like mad and the rusty razor wire is screaming and the beast is doing its head in trying to get at us. It has this desperate snarling bark that sounds all frayed like it's been used too much. It's making loud snorting, slobbering sounds and its front paws are like shovels as it tries to dig a hole under the fence.

"Bit it right off," sniggers Airplane Kev.

I say, "So he wasn't wearing any trousers then?"

"No," Airplane Kev replies after a moment.

"Why not?" I ask him. "Was it a hot day?"

Bod's now sniggering like two deflating tires.

"He must've been trying to piss on its nose or something. Yeah."

I think, *You certainly are not the sharpest tool in the box, Inflatable Kev*. But I say, "Over or under, Airplane Kev?"

"Yeah," he says, sounding chunky.

"Which is it? Weeing over the fence or weeing under the fence, Airplane Kev?"

"I don't remember."

I now try not to think about just how much of a plank poor Airplane Kev really is. I say, "Probably under."

"Under?" he asks.

"Over would mean standing on someone's shoulders. That or not having a pee for about a week before." I glance over my shoulder. "Jet propulsion." I feel bad as soon as I say it but not too bad.

Bod is now sounding like a punctured bouncy castle. And I can tell Airplane Kev has lost track of what's going on. Like, he's suddenly flown into a cloud bank or something. "Just do it," he says, and then because he can't think of anything else, "Finn would."

And you can just tell he's sorry he's said it. But it is out there and he can't take it back.

I suddenly feel two things about Airplane Kev at the same time. I feel very sorry for him but really angry with him, too. I don't know if that makes sense but it's true. Yeah. Part of me wants to tell him not to worry about it but the other bit wants to thump him with something and run. But I don't because he'd murder me in a second. Instead I have a picture of me thumping him like Itchy and Scratchy. And now I'm glad I'm looking at the fence because I definitely don't want Airplane Kev or Bod to see what's going on in my face.

I don't know why this is. I just don't.

The beast gives a last snort and I hear its heavy paws scraping on the gravel path on the other side of the fence as it goes back toward the house.

I lean toward the fence. Someone has written *arse* on it in black marker. And they've even drawn one beside it for people who don't know what an arse looks like.

Then I give it a little shake.

Nothing.

I shake it a bit harder and the rusty razor wire grumbles a bit.

Still nothing.

I'm trying not to hold my breath because I heard people can just drop down dead from doing it in stress situations like this. As if something just flicked their Off switch.

I shake it harder

More nothing

And harder

And harder

And there's even more nothing.

Now I put my ear against it. For one second I hear the sea, then it's just the noise of my own breathing and I can smell a faint varnish smell. Now there's this slow, rubbery feeling deep in my stomach that's starting to build. This is definitely what my dad calls a PBTM when my mum's around and a potential brown trouser moment when she's not.

"Hurry up, Danny," says Airplane Kev, "we've got school not to go to." And he laughs like it's the funniest thing he's ever said. But he doesn't know the really sad thing is that it probably is. Bod just leaks some air out of his mouth.

Now I'm wondering why exactly I have my face pressed against this wobbly fence with someone's arse drawn on it.

Maybe I need a holiday away from pressing my face against things or putting bricks through them.

But I'm stuck with doing it. Stuck the same way the beast is stuck with flinging himself at things. And Airplane Kev is stuck with being Airplane Kev, definitely not the sharpest tool in the box. And Bod's stuck going hiss-hiss and hiss at anyone he can.

Yeah.

I'm stuck. The beast is stuck. And my dad's stuck counting everything. And Airplane Kev is stuck. And Bod is stuck. And everyone in the whole world is stuck. Stuck. Stuck. Stuck.

Then there's this massive roaring:

Bang!

Suddenly I'm standing about twenty feet away. The fence is shuddering and the rusty razor wire is singing like mad. Also my bum is going ten p/five p at the speed of light.

Airplane Kev can move very fast for a big kid. No one is laughing now except maybe the beast. It is going mad on the other side of the wobbly fence.

Then Bod decides to crack one off. This makes us all laugh quite a bit. It's funny because cracking them off is the only thing Bod's good at apart from going hiss-hiss and hiss. Bod can crack one off any time he wants to. You could say, "Right, crack one off in three seconds exactly." And he'll do it. The only fart thing he's no good at is impressions. The best fart impressionist of all time is Finn. Even Bod admits that if you make him.

Sometimes on Saturday mornings we'd lie in bed eating stolen Jaffa cakes and Finn would do impressions. And even though he had the top bunk, it wasn't depressing in any way.

Finn would do:

creaking door in a haunted house

a long line of marching ants

approaching sports car going away again

sole of your shoe

hissing cat

boiling an egg

and most of the theme from *Star Wars*.

Even though he couldn't do it all, it was still very good because it seemed to last for ages. He did loads more but I can't remember them right now.

Of course I turned out to be rubbish at it. I only do one impression and that's squashed duck. One time I tried to cheat by eating four packets of fig rolls the night before. I bought them with some of the birthday money Uncle Phil gave me. The results were disappointing. Uncle Phil is my dad's younger brother. He told me my dad was the demon farter in their family when they were kids. He also told me he was totally rubbish like me. So it must run in the family both ways.

I did it

Right in the middle of this good laugh I'm having I suddenly remember the brick through Old Grundy's window and his flattened stuffed otter. It hits me like a cold wave at the seaside and makes my stomach go all rubbery again. It also makes me feel really sorry because I must've been this evil window-smashing, stuffed-otter-flattening kid all along. And I didn't even know it.

I catch myself wondering if I'm allowed to laugh like I did before I knew. Or do I now have to use some kind of evil laugh like the Joker in *Batman*. The kind of evil laugh that warns your victims just as you're about to get them after you've probably been sneaking up on them for a long time. Also, am I supposed to keep being evil? And if I am, is it just in a window-smashing, otter-flattening way? I hope not.

It seems like it happened a long time ago and to someone else as well. I go a bit mad for a second because I start wondering if it really was me after all. I know it must've been me. A picture of me doing it pops into my head. It makes me feel better and worse at the same time and for the same reason.

If Airplane Kev and Bod and me were in a police lineup and they brought Old Grundy in, I'd be in trouble. He'd pick me out straightaway as the evil little sod[1] that did it. The kid who puts three-holed bricks through peoples' windows and flattens their stuffed otters.

Not Airplane Kev.

Not Bod.

No. It was me. Danny. I did it.

---

[1] His favorite thing to call kids apart from sneaky little gits.

Bunking off

"You can bunk off with us," says Airplane Kev.

"I can't," I lie. "My mum and dad are coming to see Cream Egg Crimble today."

Now this really isn't a lie even though it is. My mum and dad are going to see Cream Egg Crimble but I am going to bunk off right this second.

I'm going to bunk off for ever and ever.

I just don't want to bunk off with Airplane Kev and Bod.

I pick up my bag and get out of there.

As I walk away, I know there is a big reason I didn't want to bunk off with Airplane Kev and Bod. The reason is I know I'm going somewhere but I just don't know where to yet. But I don't want to talk about that.

Old gray pants on a washing line stretching to forever

@

At the bus stop the clouds look like a washing line of old gray underpants stretching to forever. Watching them flutter gives me a light, giggly feeling. This happens a lot. I'll be walking down a street or standing at a bus stop like I am now and I'll just notice something that'll make me want to laugh.

Anyway, I sneak a quick look to see if anyone else in the queue is smiling, but there's no one. No. All faces are pointed at the ground in a heavy Monday morning way.

I feel sort of sorry for this queue all squashed down by Monday morning.

Maybe the queue has already noticed the pants-shaped clouds and I'm the only one who finds it funny. I think about pointing it out to someone but they might just decide I'm round the bend. I don't think I could explain I only find underpants clouds a bit funny—not totally funny hilarious when you have to worry about wetting yourself. I couldn't ever say, "Look at these pants-shaped clouds because you look like you need a good laugh."

No.

Sometimes there just isn't anything you can do.

Secret laugh

I look up at the underpants clouds again because I'm becoming too worried about the queue not being able to laugh at them. But now there's also a giant flattened otter. It's lying on its back holding a brick. I can't tell if it has any holes in it or not. I don't want to think about that so I look down again. That's when I notice her.

She's about the same age as my little sister, Angela. She's holding on to a big crab hand with bright blue nails. And I just know she's noticed the cloudy pants on the washing line stretching to forever. She keeps sneaking looks up at them with her big eyes then looks down and around to see if anyone else has noticed. When she sees they're too squashed down by Monday she has a little secret laugh to herself. A secret laugh is like a bubble that gets bigger and bigger until you just can't hold it in anymore. But even though you know you can't hold it in, you have to try. Squeezing it in makes your shoulders shake up and down and it hurts and it makes you laugh even more *because* it hurts.

My mum laughs like that sometimes even though she's a grown-up. She mainly does it when my dad goes into one about being so rubbish at DIY. And the more he goes into one, the more my mum does her secret shoulder-shake laugh. She told me the reason he goes into one for being so rubbish once. She was making me help her in the garden. She said it was because his own dad, my granddad, was so good at it. He was so good at DIY he built his own coffin before he died. When my mum told me she started secret shoulder-shake laughing so much she was almost sick. I thought it was a bit weird because she always really liked my granddad Joe and cried bucket loads when he died. Anyway, when I asked her why she was laughing she said it was because she had a sudden picture in her head of my dad building *his* own coffin. She was nearly choking when she said it even though it wasn't very funny.

The strangest things in the world can make you laugh. But the best laughs are usually secret laughs.

My other car's a Porsche

We used to be like that in our house. My mum and dad always wanted to talk things through, bring things out into the open. They'd get us around the dinner table to ask what we thought, especially about important stuff like moving house or the time we needed a new car when the exhaust pipe fell out of our old one.

Don't get me wrong; most times they wouldn't listen to us. I don't blame them or anything. I mean, I wouldn't listen to me either. Finn and me voted for a sports car and they said all right. We got really excited and ticked off the days on the *Crop Circles of Europe* calendar. I even had a dream about one. It was yellow and we all went on holiday in it. Angela wasn't interested because she was too young and deaf to care. Anyway one day my mum and dad turned up in this knackered old estate. It was *yellow.* My dad had put a big sticker in the rear window that said, "My other car's a Porsche." They were even wearing their matching blue anoraks. They sat in it for ages, laughing, waving, and beeping the horn. And they kept doing it even after Finn and me stopped pressing our faces against the window and went and watched television instead.

My mum and dad can be quite tricky when they want to be.

White elephant

As I watch, the little girl does her secret shoulder-shake laugh and the big crab hand with bright blue nail varnish jerks her arm. For some reason it really wants her to stop laughing, even though she can't help it. I suddenly get this terrible feeling that, well, she'll do what it wants. Then she'll forget how funny some things can be because things like Monday morning and school and jerking arms will make her forget. Maybe it's happened to everyone in this bus queue already. Maybe I'm only just noticing it right this second.

Now all this little girl can do is make me want to see my little sister again. Because I want to show Angela the underpants clouds on the washing line to forever. And if anyone tried jerking her arm to stop her laughing, I could tell them not to. Because she's my kid sister and it's my job to do that sort of thing. As the bus arrives I start thinking about all the things that could happen to her now I won't be around anymore. I don't want to think about all those things but I can't seem to stop myself. It's like saying, "Don't think of a white elephant" to someone.

Things that could happen to Angela when I'm not here

1. Run over because she can't hear the horn
2. Falling down a well because she's lost[1]
3. Being lost forever because everyone else has forgotten how to sign
4. Being squeezed by a giant something or other
5. Being put in a home because something's happened to my mum and dad
6. Being forced to make sneakers like the poor kids my dad told me about
7. Abducted by aliens[2]
8. Forgetting to laugh at underpants-shaped clouds
9. Being left alone
10. I can't think of anything else.

---

[1] See 3.
[2] It could happen.

Scared

In about one minute I'll come to the very end of all the normal stuff I usually do.

As the bus leaves the stop I begin to feel very, very scared. It's rising through my stomach in big greasy bubbles that sort of pop in my head and make my skin tingle. Even my hair feels scared. This being scared is about a million times bigger than the beast-leaping-at-a-fence sort of being scared. The worst thing is it feels everywhere at the same time. When I look out the window, the buildings are scared gray, the bus is scared bus, and my hand is scared white. The kids all have scared faces and the grown-ups sit in a scared way.

Even the plastic seat I'm sitting on feels warm and scared.

This kind of scared makes me want to pull the

emergency brake and run home because it almost makes me believe things will be like before. It makes me think this even though I know they won't, because they can't ever be the same again. And knowing that makes me want it even more. There's something else too. Yes. A secret thing underneath being scared and all the rest. I'm almost too ashamed to admit it to you.

Here goes.

Mixed in with the being scared is a tiny little bit of being excited by it—of liking it.

I'll have to stop pretending, stop hiding inside normal Monday morning things like going to school on this bus and missing the weekend. I'll have to start being and doing outside of all that. And even though I'll have to stop pretending, even though I haven't thought about anything else past this exact second, part of me is very excited by it. Don't get me wrong—I'm so scared I feel like a chocolate with a liquid center—but that other bit's still there too—the sort of enjoying bit.

Inside this moment I'm now talking to you from is also the very end of what people know about me. Soon people I meet won't know anything about Old Grundy's otter or what happened to Finn. I'll just be some kid called Danny and I might be able to stop feeling bad all the time about everything that happened. The only thing to remind me is my face but I'll just have to get used to that.

I look up and see this man watching me. He has his head shaved with a stupid-looking beard on his chin and he looks very scary. But there's something in his face. Something peeping out from behind the scariness, something soft that makes me feel better for about a second, because it says okay. Then it's gone and he's just someone on the bus.

Backward and forward

We're coming to the school stop now and all the other kids are getting ready to get off. They all have that look on their faces. The same look you get when you're about to jump into freezing water. I know I haven't got *that* look because some of the kids are giving me sly little glances as they push toward the front of the bus.

I want to be pushing to the front of the bus, too, even though I've just remembered I haven't done my maths homework. I mean, I know it's all normal kid's stuff I'm supposed to be worried about because I am a kid. But the further I go, the more stretched all over the place I feel. So now I don't know who I am or even when I'm supposed to be getting off.

The bus makes this hissing noise as the doors snap shut. Now I'm looking over my shoulder at all the streams of kids going through the gates like toothpaste getting squeezed the wrong way.

False teeth

The city center always looks like it's been made out of Legos by someone with at least six thumbs. I try not to think about this. I've decided not to laugh unless it's for something out of the ordinary like a wave of dancing hippos or someone's false teeth shooting out of their mouth when they cough.[1]

I'm off the bus now and standing here outside all my normal Monday morning things to do. I can't think what to do next. I must admit I feel stupid standing still while everyone else is moving in and out of the Lego buildings acting like they know where they're going. I wouldn't mind knowing where I'm going. I wouldn't mind that at all.

I decide to have a think about it and start by sitting on a small metal bench just outside the bus station. I

---

[1] This happened one time we were on holiday. An old lady's teeth shot into the water from the jetty when she sneezed. They sank the way jellyfish float.

notice all the rubbish lying around where people have missed the litter bin. Anyway, I postpone having a think about what to do and start picking up the litter. It's a bit of a relief because it's simple and easy to do. The rubbish is mainly drinks cartons and crisp packets and expensive sandwich wrappers. I'm picking it up because my mum always says only scumbags drop their litter on the ground. She then immediately told me never to call anyone a scumbag even if they dropped a ton of litter on the ground. I didn't ask her why because she had her scary don't-ask-me-why look on her face. My mum really hates it when people do selfish things like drop litter and not say please or thank you. She says they're mean-spirited. She even picks litter up and runs after the offenders and tries to give it back. Then she'll come back and say something like, "They're the ones soiling the planet and they think *I'm* mad for pointing it out to them!" And she doesn't care who it is. I bet she wouldn't even care if it was a sumo wrestler or some other scary-shaped person.

Now I'm holding this last flattened orange drink carton and I've just realized something. Tidying away other peoples' rubbish for them belongs to before. When I wasn't someone who put bricks through people's windows to flatten their stuffed otters. I don't want my mum to call me a scumbag but I also can't be like before. So I drop the flattened orange carton on the ground and sit down on the metal bench for my Big Think. As I'm about to begin thinking, I notice this little old lady with a walking stick and a tiny poodle on a lead. The poodle looks blue and its nails are painted pink. At first I'm scared she might know my mum and dad because of the way she glares at me. But I don't think they're the kind of mum and dad who would know someone with a poodle with its nails painted pink. I say "Don't think" because as I've already said, they can be a bit tricky sometimes.

Anyway this little old lady stares at me out of her

crumpled-looking face, then walks over. Her poodle begins to sniff my leg as she stares. She then rummages in a big pink shopping bag with a picture of Elvis on the front. Finally she takes out a folded piece of white card with something written on it and holds it up for me to see.

It's written with a red crayon in careful curly letters. It says:

Pick it up, scumbag!!!

It even has three exclamation marks to show she means business. For a moment I don't know what she means and think she may have lost her marbles a little bit. She looks a bit mad anyway. Finally she taps the sign and says, "This means you, young man!"

"It's not mine," I say, even though she must have seen me drop it.

"I saw you," she says. She taps the sign again then adds, "I saw you drop it."

She then goes back to tapping the sign. I'm about to explain but it suddenly all seems like too much. I think about running away but even that seems too much to do at this moment. Besides it would just be too mad to be chased around the Lego buildings by a little old lady and her tiny poodle with its nails painted pink. Knowing my luck she probably has other signs in her bag like:

Come back, you scumbag!

or

Stop, police!

or

Grab that stuffed otter flattener!

I know if I try to explain, everything else will come tumbling out too. Right now, right this exact moment, if I had my own sign it would say:

Leave me alone—I'm only a kid!

I think about shouting it at this little old lady who may have lost her marbles. But I've just realized, just this second, that things never leave you alone. So I stand up, pick up the flattened drinks carton, and post it into the litter bin. I go back and sit down again. I'm finding it hard to think even though I really need to at the moment. The tiny poodle is sniffing at my leg again and I just know he's considering using it as a toilet. And if that happens I would probably lose *my* marbles completely.

The little old lady doesn't look like she's going to go. So I move to the edge of the bench because she'll probably want to sit down.

I really need to think about what to do next. But nothing is coming. I'm thinking about leaving but I don't want to because I was here first. Besides, it was me who picked up all the rubbish and posted it in the litter bin.

She sits down beside me like she's my nan or something.

"Why aren't you at school?" the little old lady finally asks me, even though I've changed out of my school uniform. She then calls her poodle and begins to feed him bits of Jaffa cake.

"I'm not a scumbag," I tell her. My voice sounds hollow and older than me. What I really mean is I'm not *that* kind of scumbag.

"I saw you drop your drinks carton."

"But it wasn't mine."

"That doesn't concern me," she says. Then in a softer voice she asks, "Why did you pick it up and then throw it down again?"

"I don't put other peoples' rubbish in litter bins for them anymore," I admit.

"Why?" she asks.

"Because," I say. And that's all I say because one

more single word might make it all spill out.

The little old lady watches all the people scooting and pinging around for a moment then says that it's sad. She says it means they've won; they've beaten me. So I say okay, okay, so they've beaten me and big deal and some other cheeky things like that. But the sound of her voice saying the word "sad" makes me feel really sad, too. And I've enough to feel sad about without taking on everything else.

"This poor old planet needs people who pick up litter," she says. "It doesn't care who does it as long as they keep doing it."

"Well, I don't do it anymore," I repeat.

"I also used to trip litterers up any chance I got," she confides.

"Were you not worried about going to jail?" I ask, interested even though I don't want to be. Thinking about what to do next is becoming like maths homework you don't want to do so you keep putting it off.

"Oh, I don't care about that at my age, dear" is all she says about that. Then, "I don't do it anymore."

"I don't think my mum trips people up." I tell her about mum chasing people and all that. Then in case she's disappointed I add, "She does call them scumbags, though."

The little old lady nods with approval. She then tells me that tripping them with her walking stick made them think a bit more.

"If Louie tries to wee on your leg, you mustn't take it at all personally, dear," she says. "It's just his way of saying hello." Then she shakes my hand with her pigeon's-foot hand and tells me her name is Carki.

"Danny," I reply, and saying it to her makes my voice shake.

Carki goes on to tell me she's a retired English teacher, then she asks me what my favorite book is. It's *Huckleberry Finn*. So I say, *"Huckleberry Finn."* It's the only book I've taken with me.

Carki tells me how Mark Twain was born the night Halley's Comet arrived and died the night it came back. I already know because my dad told me when we were reading it together. But I say, "Yeah?" because she's really enjoying telling me. And because she seems to enjoy my surprise, I repeat it a couple of times more.

Carki tells me she sees it as her duty to help us all become better people even if we don't seem to want to be. She says people probably want to be better underneath but either they've forgotten or just don't know. "Not wanting to be a better person is just too mad to contemplate," she says. She then rummages around in her Elvis shopping bag and shows me some of her signs.

Carki's Signs

Saying please and thank you
doesn't hurt anyone!!!

and

You! Yes, you! Please switch off that mobile
phone while you're driving!!!

and

How would you like me to come around to
your house and do that???

and

Buying a lot of rubbish doesn't buy
your children's love!!![1]

and

Aliens abound!!![2]

---

[1] I'm not sure about that one.
[2] I don't ask.

Big small-dog poos

When Carki finishes showing me her signs, we don't say anything for a while. Then Louie the tiny poodle jumps up and starts doing this mad around and around dance before finally settling down to do the biggest small-dog poo I've ever seen. And he just keeps doing it and doing it for ages. Louie the poodle who put the poo into poodle.

"It's the Jaffa Cakes," Carki explains. She then rummages in her Elvis shopping bag and takes out a plastic bag and a small blue seaside shovel. So I start thinking, *Please don't ask me, please don't ask me, please don't ask me* about a million times before she asks,

"Would you mind awfully dear? It's my back."

I look at the poo and think, *No wonder you've got a sore back.*

Just because . . .

I do mind shoveling the dog poo but I do it anyway.
I don't say anything while I'm doing it until Carki
says, "*Now* seems like a good time to tell me why
you're here." She smiles. "It'll take your mind off
things, dear."

I look down at what Louie's just done and hope
she's right.

It all comes out when I'm shoveling up Louie the
poodle's giant poo.

And I tell her:

because there's nothing else to do

because I haven't really spoken since what
    happened to Finn

because she's lost some of her marbles

because I've lost some of my marbles

because it feels like practice

because I'm shoveling up Louie the little blue
poodle's giant poo

because I'm running away and I'm never, ever
coming back

and well, just because . . .

When I've finished, I understand two things.
The first thing is this: Whatever I do it will never
go away no matter what. Because for a second there
I felt it empty out of me like it was gone for good
but now it's slowly filling me up again.

The second thing is why Louie the tiny poodle
looks so tired all the time.

When I come back from the dog toilet, Carki's
feeding Louie the tiny poodle another Jaffa cake.
As I sit down I wonder if she's had time to write a
new cardboard sign about stuffed otter flattening.
But instead she says, "You did the right thing,
dear."

"But I broke his window," I explain because it's
not what I expected her to say. And now I'm a bit

worried she doesn't realize how evil I am.

Carki goes on to tell me about all the countless things being broken every single moment of the day. Things a lot more important than a window belonging to a silly old duffer like Grundy. It's hard to know if all this mad stuff she's going on about is true. I mean, I'm only this kid, after all. Things are a lot more mixed-up and scary now than they were when I was nine or eight or seven or whatever. Also I haven't been ten for very long so I'm probably not very good at it yet. That's a big problem for me about most things. By the time I get used to them, they change. When I try to explain some of this to Carki she says most people are mixed-up and confused by things but just pretend they're not.

"Even my dad?" I ask her. She nods but I find it very hard to believe even though I know there must be lots of stuff he doesn't know about. Besides, my dad would never pretend to know more than he does. He likes people who are not afraid to ask about things. Sometimes, though, he thinks you want to know a lot more about something than you really do. So you end up nodding and nodding and nodding until Mum comes and rescues you or you pretend you're bursting to go to the toilet or something like that. My dad says a lot of people spend most of their time going around pretending they know stuff. He says they spend more time worrying about looking stupid than learning something new. Even *I* know how stupid that is.

While I'm thinking about all this, Carki gives me two Jaffa Cakes. She says I can have one but I'd better secret-eat it pretty quick or Louie will definitely hold it against me. I just go ahead and feed him both because I can't stand the idea of even a tiny blue poodle with pink sparkly nails not liking me. When you're running away you need all the friends you can get.

Anyway, right about now Carki says, "You don't look like someone who's running away, dear."

Then when I ask her what I do look like, she says, "To be totally honest I'm not sure, dear. Maybe you're running toward something."

"But I've no idea where I'm going," I tell her.

"The important thing is that you're going, dear," she says. "Sometimes these things take care of themselves."

Now I do the nod and nod and nod thing because I haven't a clue what she's on about.

Finally she says, "When people nod a great deal they're usually telling you they don't know something, dear."

"I don't know," I admit. And saying it makes me feel better.

Carki smiles.

"Have another Jaffa cake."

As soon as I take it, I feel Louie the tiny blue poodle give me a filthy look.

I give him half.

Then a man walks past talking loudly into a

mobile phone. He drops a paper coffee cup on the ground, squashes it, then walks on. As she and Louie take off after him, Carki shouts over her shoulder, "Suits are the very worst! Good luck, Danny dear." As she goes she tugs out a sign from her Elvis shopping bag that says:

Pick up your litter, you ignorant lout!
Yes!
This means you!!!

I watch Carki and Louie vanish after the litterbug. And I feel very sorry for lying to her.

Marbles

As I wander though the city center I start thinking about the things Carki said to me. I always thought you had to know where you were going for the going to make any sense. All around me people seem to know where they're going. I mean, even if it's just going in and out of shops. Then I start to notice how strange it all looks: all those people who know where they're going and all the shops they're going in and out of. Well, they're all part of the same strangeness. People are just smaller parts and the shops are just bigger. Then suddenly I realize I need to go to all the places Finn and me went to together. And as soon as I think this thought something really mad happens.

I hear him calling. . . .

Boo!!!

Even though he only says one word, I hear his voice very clearly. It comes out of all the people moving around and around the Lego-shaped shops buying stuff. It's very close and clear like he's just whispered in my ear this very second. It has that underneath sound to it Finn always used when he wanted to get me to laugh at something, something he didn't want anyone else to know about or laugh at. I feel jumpy—the way you feel for a second when someone jumps out at you and shouts BOO!!! So you don't know whether to laugh or thump them one. I look for Finn inside the moving people. I look even though I know it isn't him because it can't be him because it'll never be him again.

Then Finn's voice shouts, "ANGELA!"

His voice is so loud I can't understand why no

one else can hear it. And now I know I need to see Angela again before I go. And it doesn't feel like I'm using that to hide from going away for a little bit longer. I'm not hiding now because I sort of know where I'm going to after I've gone and seen Angela. And even if I don't know what to do after *that*, well, I don't care because it hasn't even happened yet.

The duvet of shame

I don't have to catch the bus back to Holt Street or anything depressing like that. My mum always takes Angela to the Institute for the Deaf on Monday mornings. They go to signing classes and then to the park and the playground. It's part of their normal Monday morning thing to do. Dad, Finn, and me used to go with them to the institute on Saturdays. It was part of the big plan to make us a signing family. My mum came up with the idea and my dad went along with it. My dad tends to go along with most of the stuff my mum asks him to do, even the stuff you can see he really doesn't want to do.[1] He'll get really angry for a while but usually end up doing it anyway. He will then try to ruin it for her by whispering rude stuff in her ear. But my mum doesn't listen until she karate chops him on

---

[1] The Festival of Childhood jumps to mind. It's this thing with crafts and handmade shoes and boring wooden games.

the arm. This is her sign for my dad to stop. Really big domestics usually end up with one of them[2] sleeping on the settee under the duvet of shame—as my dad calls it. The duvet of shame is covered in a big explosion of yellow sunflowers. Big Nan bought it for us at a car boot sale one time even though everyone protested about it. My mum even begged her not to buy it. We all hate it including Angela even though she's deaf. Big Nan may have done it for a laugh but it's hard to tell.

Anyway, having to go to signing classes wasn't all that bad even if it meant learning stuff outside school. It became a sort of secret language between Finn and me while at the same time being good for teaching Angela rude words. Doing that was more fun than you'd think. A lot of times it was even better when she got them wrong. And as long as it wasn't really rude words—words I can't even say now—Mum and Dad didn't seem to mind. That took the fun out of it a bit but not too much. Angela

---

[2] Usually him

learned how to sign really quickly. My dad says it's because she doesn't have to think about it first the way the rest of us have to do. He says ours (people who can hear) is only one way of thinking about things. He says there are lots of other ways we can't even begin to understand. There is no better or worse kind of learning. It's all just learning. My dad says even a dung beetle's view of the world is something we can never understand. I don't think it's too hard to work out what a dung beetle thinks about. After all, it isn't called a dung beetle for nothing. When I said this to my dad I could tell from his face I wasn't getting what he meant. This tends to happen a lot.

Cheesy Wotsits

In my opinion the best sandwich in the world ever is made of Cheesy Wotsits. It doesn't matter what kind of bread you use, though brown is better for you. That's what I'm eating at the moment as I walk along toward the park. A Cheesy Wotsit sandwich. I made them last night when everyone else had gone to bed. I know I should save them but I didn't eat much breakfast because my belly felt like rubber.

I really need to do a wee. I go to the toilet a lot. In fact, I go so much my dad said he was going to start charging me. At first I wasn't sure if he was joking because sometimes he doesn't smile when he's winding me up. If my mum's around when he's doing it she might save me. Sometimes she won't, though, if she thinks it's funny. My dad spends a lot of time in the toilet. So much so my mum said she was thinking about charging *him*. He built a small bookshelf in the upstairs loo because he likes to be in there for about a million years. He put the shelf up because he said he was bored reading the back of toothpaste tubes. My mum put up a big fight about it because she thought it would encourage Finn and me to be like him. She stopped when he said he'd put the shelf in the downstairs toilet instead. My mum said that would be even worse because it's near the kitchen. Anyway there's a good selection of books and even my mum leaves hers there for when she's having a soak.

When I get to the park I go straight to the toilets but they're closed because someone's wrecked them. So I go behind the bushes, walking funny because I need to go so much. And it comes pouring out for ages and ages and is very loud. But it isn't steamy because it's not that cold. A gray squirrel scoots down a tree and watches me for a bit. It gives me a dirty squirrel look for weeing on its squirrel home. I tell it I'm sorry and explain about the public toilet being closed and wrecked and all. I also point out it could have been worse, all things considered. It could've been a poo. Now I feel stupid talking to a squirrel while doing a wee but I'm only doing it to keep my mind away from being scared about being caught weeing. As you probably know, when you're nervous sometimes you can't go. My Uncle Phil told me he sings "Bohemian Rhapsody" when he can't go.

I can't do that because I don't know all the words, and besides I don't really like Queen anyway. It would be just my luck to get caught. I can imagine the newspaper headlines:

EVIL OTTER FLATTENER CAUGHT
WHIZZING ON GRAY SQUIRREL'S HOME!!!

Carki and Louie the tiny blue poodle would probably have to write a completely new sign.

Duck

I don't get caught but I do manage to wee on the toes of my sneakers. It happened because my nervous laugh went off without warning. Thinking about Carki's new sign made it happen. I walk through the park toward the iron bridge that lets you cross the river. Even though it was raining earlier, the river is low and slow moving. During the winter the water level rose so high it was almost touching the walkway.

There are some people feeding the overweight ducks. It's mainly women and little kids so I have to make sure Mum and Angela aren't there. Sometimes feeding the ducks is part of their Monday morning thing to do together. Sometimes when she gets bored Angela throws the bread crusts at the ducks instead. And they're so big and fat they can't move as fast as their skinnier relations. And she's become a really good shot. Sometimes my mum gets annoyed but the ducks don't seem to mind.

Bouncing stale bread crusts off fat, greedy ducks' heads is one of the very last things Finn and me taught Angela to do. And as I think about this, I realize I know something. And it's a big something that's been hiding inside me all along. It's been waiting to pop out this very second. If something absolutely has to be the very last thing you'll ever get to teach someone, you could do a lot worse than teaching them to bounce stale bread off fat, greedy ducks' heads. Well, it makes me feel a bit better about things. And to be honest, right this second I don't care if you think I deserve to feel better or not.

On the other side of the iron bridge someone's done a big carving out of an old tree trunk. It's like a big fat cigar some giant's stuck in the ground. Two otters are sort of swirling down around the outside chasing a big fish. The only problem is someone has broken off the first otter, the one at the top. Where it was swirling down, there's nothing left but a rough, jagged bit like an ugly scar. The otter at the bottom looks a bit sad and lonely now even though it's just about to catch a big fat fish in half a second. It's sad because it would've liked to share some of the big fish it's about to catch. Only now it'll never get the chance. Because that other otter, the one at the top, is gone for good. He's never coming back.

A lot of the kids from the institute come to the playground part of the park. Even from a distance you can see them signing away to each other as they whiz around all over the place. Sometimes on good weather days the parents have a picnic together as if they're part of a club or something. I'm hoping it'll happen today even though it's been raining.

I don't go into the playground. Instead I hide behind a tree trunk outside the iron railings. I try to avoid pretending to be 007 or anything like that, even though I am spying on people and I don't want to get caught. It'd be too distracting.

The part of the fence near me has become the lost glove department with about ten single gloves lined on the top of the railing from the winter. They look like they're waving, but not in a "Hello how are you?" kind of way. It's more like a "Help! Help! Get me out of here" kind of wave. A sort of *drowning* wave, if you know what I mean.

I see my mum almost at once because she's the only deaf kid mum with mad red hair. Angela has mad red hair too but she's harder to see because she's tiny and always wears a brown monkey hat. She's worn it since she was three because Irish Nan knitted it for her third birthday. She'd throw a massive strop if you even mentioned in passing that she should leave it behind for once. Angela can be very loud for a deaf kid. Mum says it's because she has no volume control.

You can never know for one single second what someone is going to care suddenly about.[1]

Finally I spot her. She's waiting in a queue of other little deaf kids for her go on the biggest slide in the playground. And of course she's wearing her brown monkey hat.

Now as I watch Angela wait her turn to go up the giant slide, I start feeling bad for her all over again. I mean, she doesn't even realize for a moment just how tiny she really is and just how big everything else is around her. I mean it's like this:

Angela

---

[1] Or why

Every-
thing
else

She's telling some other deaf kid with one long eyebrow over her eyes like a yellow caterpillar about Donut running into the kitchen table again. Her little hands are moving like mad. I don't think the other little deaf kid with the yellow caterpillar can keep up because she keeps signing, *What? And what? And what?*

Just as Angela is repeat-telling her just how really stupid Donut is, another kid shoves into her from behind and knocks her flying. He has his back turned. But he's really big and Angela bounces off him. I want to scoot right over the lost glove department railing and help her up and thump him one. Even though I know he doesn't mean it. I mainly want to show him just how big he is and tell him how he should spend every minute of his waking life watching out for tiny little creatures like my kid sister. It's my job.

Then Angela gets up and goes straight over and shoves the big kid back. I really mean it. She gives herself a bit of a run at him then shoves him as hard as she can. It doesn't do much and she bounces off him but she does get his attention. When he turns around she signs: "Bog off, you stupid git!"

I feel two things about this. One is being proud because Finn and me taught her to. The second is a full-on ten p/five p feeling. Because to him she's just this tiny little kid in a silly-looking brown monkey hat who's just shoved him and signed something rude, too. And you don't have to be able to read sign to know it's rude. I can see him thinking about thumping her, but he doesn't because she's too small and his mates would laugh. Then it's over because the kid with the yellow caterpillar eyebrow nudges Angela, as it's her turn to whiz down the giant slide. She goes scampering up the steep mountain made of metal steps, then comes rocketing down the slide at the speed of light.

It's just too mad that she doesn't realize how easy she is to break.

Things that could happen to Angela on the giant slide

1. She could slip on the step where some other kid's spilt their drink.

2. She could tumble back down the steel steps on her head.

3. She could catch her foot on the top rail and dangle until the fire brigade comes.

4. She could fall off the top and land outside the soft safety bit.

5. She could slide down too fast and land on her knees.

6. She could slide down too slow and be kicked in the back by someone going faster.

7. She could get stuck and crushed by the pileup.

8. She could be tripped at the bottom.

9. She could be flattened by someone falling.[1]

10. The slide could fall on her.

[1] See 4.

And the thing that scares me the most is it will happen to her in the exact same way that big clumsy kid happened to her. He came out of the blue and he didn't even know he'd done it. And even though he didn't mean to, she was knocked over just the same. Angela could get broken by something that doesn't even know it's broken her. I mean, most things that can happen won't give an evil laugh first or anything like that. It might be better if they did because at least it would be a bit of a warning. At least that would be something.

And Angela acts like none of this has anything to do with her, as if it's not her problem. And it's not even as if she could hear an evil warning laugh anyway. As I watch her come shooting down the slide again it hits me like a brick just how little and easy to flatten just like that she could be.

I look over at my mum and wonder if she knows about any of this. She's standing by a red swing being all small and ginger. I heard her tell my dad once that she found it hard to look like a real mum should look. I think she meant mums off the telly or in *Take-a-Break* magazine. Anyway she's standing beside three other mums who do look like real mums stepped off the telly or out of *Take-a-Break* magazine. I can tell by the way she's standing she's probably wondering how to look like those other three real mums.

Sometimes my mum does things you wouldn't think a real mum would do. One of the things she does is draw comic pictures of what happens in our family. She keeps them locked up in a big suitcase so I suppose it's a sort of diary. I don't think the drawings are in any order in the suitcase but she does always put the date in the bottom left-hand corner. She also always uses the exact same sort of pen.

My favorite drawing is from when I was eight. It was about me coming in with a big ice cream. She looked at me funny for a minute then said she'd give me two quid if I'd let her stick my ice cream in my face. I said yes because I could buy about three more with that much money and still get to keep what was left of the wrecked one. She told me to take the flake out in case it put my eye out. When she did it she had this big inside grin on her face. Then when she pushed the ice cream cornet on to my nose, she started laughing because it stuck there like Pinocchio when he was caught lying. Even though the ice cream was cold and it went up both my nostrils and made my nose numb I didn't mind. Because when she'd finished she said thanks and that it had made her feel a lot better about things. And that was good to know. Later I split the money with Finn but we didn't buy any ice cream. I think we bought crisps. I was still digging bits of hardened ice cream and raspberry ripple out of my nose for a couple of days afterwards. It sort of put me off for a while.

Argentina

man are anxiously replies that because he's in hot stuff and repeatedly shakes as, and if Rumsey normally can't stand me because she's hopelessly unstable. My dad

As I look at my mum standing in the playground beside those other real-looking mums, something about her seems to become smaller. This has been happening a lot recently. The whole world has stayed the same but everyone I know seems to have shrunk. Suddenly it feels like everyone I worry about could be flattened by a giant slide at any second without warning. Another thing I can tell just by looking over at my shrinking mum is she doesn't know she's shrinking. So I suppose no one else knows either.

Anyway, just looking like a real mum doesn't mean you are one. I know this because of a boy in my class at school called Tony Rumsey. He's the kind of boy who goes to Euro Disney for his holidays and maybe somewhere else, too. We're not mates or anything like that because all his mates always dress up in new stuff and expensive sneakers all the time. Rumsey normally can't stand me because I'm a charity shop casualty kid. My dad said his ambition is never to buy anything new ever again. The only thing my mum won't buy out of chazzers is underpants. Because that would just be too depressing to even think about.

So you can see why it came as a bit of a surprise when Tony Rumsey started talking to me one morning. I must admit I was glad to have someone to talk to because they'd just split Finn and me up from each other. It was because when we were together we were what Cream Egg Crimble called "disruptive elements." School isn't much fun when you can't sign to each other or take turns pretending to fall off your chair ten times each in thirty-five minutes or make pretend fart noises with your armpits or do real farts. Anyway, the morning I'm talking about, Tony Rumsey was dropped off by his very real-looking mum in one of those giant four-wheel-drive Jeeps my dad hates so much. Rumsey marched right up to me. At first I thought he was going to thump me one because he'd finally snapped and couldn't bear even the very idea of my continuing existence. He had this mad look on his face and, as I've said, he normally can't stand me. But this morning he just said, "Danny or Finn?" in a strange, wobbly voice. I told him who I was and he said, "Do you like Argentina?"

I was a bit surprised so I said I hadn't really thought about it but I was sure it was okay anyway. Then he said, "Guess where I spent the night last night?"

So I had to say, "I don't know, where did you spend the night last night?"

"In our cellar," he said with a sniggery little laugh that made me think of a mad gerbil.

"Were you camping?" I was having to try very hard not to laugh at the word "gerbil" because I always thought it sounded so stupid.

"No," he sniggered, "but I just bet it's bigger than yours anyway."

I said it probably was because our cellar is quite tiny and my dad keeps his home brew down in it.

So it went on like that, being just too mad for first thing in the morning in the school playground. Then he rolled up the sleeve of his hoody and showed me this big purple bruise on his arm. And I swear it was the exact same shape as Argentina. At first I thought he was showing me because he was quite proud of it. But he had this look on his face that had nothing to do with being proud. Then it all came out of him like he was puking up or something. And it felt like he was shrinking even though he actually stayed the exact same size.

Rumsey told me his mum had lost most of her marbles even though she was the most real-looking mum I've ever seen. He told me she spent a lot of the time sleeping or crying or shouting or burning dinner or locking him in the cellar because he couldn't eat the dinner she'd incinerated. He told me this time it was because he took the blame for wetting the bed[1] so his kid sister wouldn't get locked in the cellar all night. He just went on puking out words like he couldn't stand the taste of them.

And before you think I'm giving anything away, I'm not. The way he said it all to me didn't sound he wanted it to be secret. He sounded like he was saying it to no one in particular. He could've been saying it to me or the litter bin or the whole wide world. To tell the truth I got the feeling he was only standing beside me because the rubbish bin smelled a bit. I didn't understand why he had to puke out all those words at the time, but now I'm telling you this I think I understand it a tiny little bit. I think Rumsey just needed to say it so it wouldn't just be locked up inside his head all the time. I was just the next step up from a smelly old rubbish bin in a school playground. Anyway, as he walked away he turned and said, "I've never liked you."

---

[1] Finn did that for a while even though he had the top bunk.

Muddled up

Even though my mum isn't a very real-looking mum, I still think she's a very good mum. She's never locked us in the cellar or incinerated our dinner—well, not very often. Now that I come to think about it, she'll probably start to think she's even less of a real mum now I'm doing this bunk. Just thinking that makes me feel all crumpled up inside like an old chip wrapper.

Muddled up

Muddled up for Mum

Muddled up for Dad

Muddled up for Angela

Muddled up.

I can't seem to remember a time when things weren't all muddled up. Even the stuff from before it happened to Finn, clear stuff you wouldn't think was muddled up in any way, it can't escape it, either. Now it feels like it was just waiting for a chance to be muddled up all along. Very sneaky, very sneaky indeed.

I mean, even the strongest things in the world, things that have already safely happened, only look strong and safe and happened. They only seem like they're standing still, but they're not. No. Nothing stands still, not even for one single second. And what's more, not standing still usually means getting broken. Most of the world is like that, ready to burst into one million pieces at the drop of a hat, and there's nothing you can do about it.

Thinking about all this stuff has made me feel so rotten inside the only thing I want to do is sit behind a tree and eat my last Cheesy Wotsit sandwich.[1]

---

[1] There are other kinds now such as Smoky Bacon but Cheesy is best for sarnies. (I also have an emergency packet but that's for emergencies.)

1. They can buy a smaller car that's kinder to the environment.
2. They can go on better holidays.
3. They can rent out our room.
4. They can stop thinking about Finn.
5. They can stop thinking about Danny.[1]
6. They won't be reminded of anything or anyone anymore.

---

[1] See 6.

I don't ever want to be a grown-up. You have to always be so bloody miserable. I mean, there's enough to worry about being a kid. When you're finally grown-up, there's millions more. There are bills and car insurance and finding a job before you even get near to worrying about people and the state of the world.

My dad says if there's a god he must have a very sick sense of humor. To tell the truth, I never knew what he meant until the thing with Finn. But now I think he means that God sticks you with having to worry about all the people you have to worry about. He makes them really easy to flatten, then shoves them in a big, big world where there are millions of things just waiting to flatten them.

I don't know about you but when I stop and

think about it, I'm scared. Scared in the background like a radio playing. Most of the time you don't notice it but every now and then you do. Every now and then it leaps out to sort of get you when you're not expecting it.

I mean, apart from people, I worry about:
Huckleberry Finn,
ice cream,
swimming,
farts,
pickled onion monster munch,
kung-fu films,
birthdays,
holidays,
and Cheesy Wotsit sandwiches.
To tell the truth I'm scared stiff of all the things we used to share because they must've been so easy to break all along and I just didn't know it.

Bubbles (part one)

Now I think about it, I sort of know why people are always running around all over the place all the time. I think they're always trying to run away from being background scared. It's as if by running away from it is a kind of pretending it isn't there, that it isn't chasing you.

It starts as soon as you know people don't last.

As I said, I've only noticed it since what happened to Finn. So maybe it takes something really big to make it jump out on you the first time. It was a bit worrying to realize that Mum and Dad must've been background scared all along. I was always used to thinking about them in the same way as superheroes like the Incredible Hulk. You know, impossible to flatten in any way except for perhaps some super-secret way.

I follow Mum and Angela for a little bit when they leave the playground. I do it because I want to hang on to every single little detail about them. I don't ever want to forget what they look like. I walk behind them, staring until my eyes begin to sting from making myself not blink in case I miss anything.

They walk hand in hand like a lot of other people seem to be doing. Sometimes Mum will point at things so Angela can notice them too. I know Mum always squeezes her hand to get her attention before she points at something interesting. It's one of the ways they share things. It keeps them inside their own private bubble. Looking across the park I can see that they're surrounded by loads of other private bubbles. The bubbles are all different. But the thing they have in common is at least two people inside or at least two living things like Carki and Louie the tiny blue poodle.

I don't have a private bubble anymore because I'm on my own.

When Mum and Angela come to the diving otter sculpture, they stop for a minute. I must admit it makes me feel strange watching them like this. It's because I know what they're missing because I'm missing it too. Feeling the exact same thing they're feeling at the exact same time makes me feel sort of close to them, even though I'm standing way over here by the trees. I feel close enough to hold their hands.

Laughing shed

On Saturday morning I think I said good-bye to Angela but you can't ever be sure with her. My mum says she's deep as the ocean.

Anyway, Mum was in bed. Something she does a lot now. Dad was downstairs watching something about the planets. I didn't go near him, because it would've been one of those things he would've made Finn and me watch with him.

I came out into the back garden to look at the brick with three holes I was going to dig up. Angela was busy getting Donut to run into the shaky garden shed to make it shake. She was bouncing his chewy ball close enough to make him skid into it. She looked happy the door was rattling, even though she couldn't hear it.

Donut was having a really good laugh. Each time

he banged into the shed, he brought his chewy ball back for her to throw again. And even though it was covered in slime, she kept doing it anyway.

She suddenly looked small and mad and sad all at the same time. She was wearing her Halloween witch's dress that was supposed to look scary. But with her monkey hat, it just made her look really easy to flatten.

I knew she knew something was going to happen. She'd been following me around for the last few days and she'd given me all these sneaky looks. They were sneaky because she'd look away every time I looked back.

I waited by the garden path until she couldn't stop herself from giving me a sneaky look, then I signed, *Can I have a go?*

Angela stopped making Donut bang into the shed for a moment to think about it. But it wasn't normal windup making me wait. She was really thinking about it.

Then she started making Donut bang into the shed again.

So I had to wait for her to sneaky look at me again. I could see she was trying hard not to. When she finally did I signed, *Please, Angela*.

Donut stopped banging into the shaky shed again for a moment. I think she was going to pretend she didn't understand.[1] But she didn't; she just went back to making Donut bang into the shaky shed.

By that point the shed was shaking so much it looked like it was laughing.

I felt so bad for the both of us that I turned to go back to the house. But I didn't get more than three or four steps when this wet, squelching thing thumped me when it hit the back of the head. And it was so covered in glop, it splatted on the ground.

I turned around and Angela was standing there beside Donut whose tail was wagging like mad.

---

[1] She's really good at that.

Now I get the feeling that it's the right time to go. I know if I stay here in the park any longer I won't be able to stop myself from going over to Angela and Mum. This is because if I can't save them from being flattened, at least I can get flattened with them.

But I don't go over to them. No. I just walk away through all the other people caught up inside their own personal bubbles. I sneak one more secret look at Mum and Angela over my shoulder. They've left the wrecked diving otter sculpture and walked across the iron bridge. They're pointing and sign-ing and holding hands again. They're slowly moving their private bubble away to catch the number fifty-seven bus home. My mind starts to imagine what they'll think when they find out I've gone, but I can't look at that yet.

Bubbles (part three)

Oh yes, another thing about bubbles is they burst, that's how you know they're bubbles.

Pigeons

I always feel sorry for the pigeons at train stations. They always act like they want to be your friend all the time. I know it's because they're probably just looking for something to eat. But without trying too hard, you can imagine they're there to meet you or something. My dad says some people call them flying rats because they'll poo on anything, given half a chance.

They must be really stupid to hang around in a big station like this. I mean, there's loads of hints and signs to tell them they're not wanted. If you think like a pigeon for a second, you realize that someone has put sharpened wire spikes anywhere you'd really want to sit. Spikes designed to stick up your bum. It must be really rotten to be so not wanted that people are happy to stick wire spikes up your bum. The pigeons don't seem to mind, though, because they're probably too stupid.

I've bought my ticket with the last of my birthday money and now I'm waiting for my train. The man who sold me my ticket looked really blurred and miserable behind his thick glass screen. I've never thought about it before, but it must make you feel blurred and miserable to just sit there while you have to sell people tickets to all over the place.

The things I'm feeling inside right now:

Not knowing what will happen next

Feeling like I'm going on holiday

Leaving it all behind and never coming back

The feeling of moving deep in my belly

Excitement at going on a big train by myself

Scared of going on a big train by myself

Worried about the people I worry about

Worried about being caught by the police

Having nowhere to go

Wanting a Cheesy Wotsit sandwich.

Supposed

Because I've come so far outside my normal Monday morning things to do, it's really hard to know the right thing to feel about it all. When you're inside your normal things to do, you know what to feel. That's because you've usually done it a lot and people have told you or shown you. Not just your parents or other grown-ups, but your friends, too. I mean at the bus stop, you're *supposed* to be bored. When you realize you've forgotten to do some homework, you're *supposed* to feel a bit sick. When a big dog crashes against a fence you're standing near, your bum is *supposed* to go ten p/five p.

Stuff like that.

When the train finally comes into the platform, it rumbles like a rhinoceros. I'm glad it's a great big, loud train because they really make you know you're going somewhere. I mean, why would they bother with a big train if you weren't going somewhere big. My dad showed me a photograph of a train once that was about five miles long. It was in America somewhere. My dad really loves trains. One time he gave Finn and me his old Hornby set from when he was a kid. We played with it for a bit but got bored. Then we realized you could make the trains have head-on collisions or flatten the animals from our Playmobil farm. But after a while that got boring, too. My dad explained this was because between us we didn't have the attention span of a gnat. Then when we didn't say anything for a minute or so he explained that a gnat was a very small fly. Then Finn asked him if Play Stations ran on steam[1] when he was a kid. Dad laughed because the age of steam was one million years ago. When he laughed, I wished I'd said it.

---

[1] He made us watch a video on steam trains from the library before he gave the train set.

Clockwork

Now I'm walking down the platform. Now I'm climbing up into the train. Now I'm thinking about putting my bag on the luggage rack because other people are doing it, including some kids. Now I decide not to because I want to read *Huckleberry Finn* and I have some apples and something to drink in my bag. Now I find a seat facing the same way the train is going because I always do this no matter what. I feel funny not being able to see where I'm going. Now I realize I really need the toilet again but can't go because we're still in the station. Now I'm thinking about the wee going out along the track and wondering what happens to the poo.

The reason why I've said *now* and *now* and *now* is to show you how clockwork I'm feeling inside.

The reason I'm feeling clockwork is because all those feelings slithering around inside me like snakes have stopped slithering. They've gone away somewhere and I hope they're happy. It's like they got fed up because I couldn't work out which one to feel properly.

Now the big engine begins to vibrate the carriage and this big I-don't-know-where-I'm-going feeling suddenly pours through me. It makes me stop being clockwork. Instead it turns me into someone who could poo himself at any second. I'm not background scared anymore, either. I'm sitting-in-the-seat-next-to-me scared instead. I'm shaky scared the way you get before you go into the dentist.

This is the farthest I've ever been away from home on my own ever. And even though I know I'm here and the seat feels soft and the window feels cold and flat when I put my face against it, it isn't real. It feels like someone else's train journey and they're just telling me about it. I take *Huckleberry Finn* and try to read the bit where Huck and Jim first set off. But the words just look like black marks and they won't have anything to do with me.

Shopping bag creature

This boy comes shooting down the aisle toward me. It's like he's being chased by something that really wants to eat him. He sort of reminds me of the spoon from the dish and spoon rhyme because his head is too big for his tiny little body. I instantly feel sorry for him without knowing why. And even though he's going so fast, he manages not to bump into any of the other passengers who're still putting their luggage away in the overhead racks. Then I see what's chasing him. It's a big, bulging shopping bag creature. One of those rubbish aliens you find in cheesy monster films. The ones where everyone runs around screaming too much.

The spoon-faced boy scoots into the seat opposite me. He keeps that being-chased look on his face even after the creature chasing him turns into his mum, huff-puffing her heavy shopping on to the table. That chased look sticks like it belongs there. Then his mum dumps a big fat shopping bag full of frozen chicken parts on *Huckleberry Finn*. This immediately makes me not want to like her, even though my mum says you should always give people a chance. I don't like her because before she plopped her bag down she saw the book lying there and just didn't care.

Anyway, they both stand on my feet and don't say sorry.[1]

---

[1] My mum says good manners don't cost anything.

Sausages

Alien-mum also has a spoon-shaped head but you wouldn't really notice unless you stared for a minute or so. Because it's big like the rest of her is big. Maybe she's chased and caught and eaten a lot of kids. When she sits she sort of sucks everything in, then lets it out again. She does it in a way that gives me the feeling that the world is always several sizes too small for her. And she smells like the dentist's.

Then I notice she has really tiny hands. You can't believe how small they look hanging there at the ends of her bigness. Her fingers are just like those little sausages you can eat one hundred of before you get sick. It's like she picked them up by mistake and left her own fingers behind. This thought makes me (secret) laugh a bit. She is wearing a lot of rings and her nails are painted pink the same as Louie the blue poodle's.

The spoon-faced boy immediately begins to stare out the window. But he's careful not to press his face against the glass, which I think is one of the best things you can do at the start of a trip. He stares without blinking even though we haven't left the station yet. Even though there's nothing to see except gray concrete walls and big black smears of soot. I don't look because out of the corner of my eye I've just noticed that the biggest soot smear is suspiciously otter shaped. And to be honest I'd rather not see another otter for a little while.

I use the boy's station staring to have a really good look at him without being noticed. His eyes are shaped a bit like alien's eyes. They are slightly flattened dark circles.

I stare at him for so long his head starts to look false like he can take it off any time he wants. Just like a Doctor Zargle[1] alien can when it comes down

---

[1] Angela's favorite book

to earth to secretly study our ways. And all the time I'm staring at him, my feeling-sorry feeling is getting bigger and bigger. Then I notice how tidy looking he is. Not like the normal clean and tidy sneak attack your mum does on you before you go out somewhere. No, it's the clean and tidy you only get from sitting completely still all the time and never touching anything. Then I notice he has this mad name label pinned on his sweater under his coat which must be in case he gets lost or forgets his name or something like that. But I don't have time to see what it says because Alien-mum's just caught me staring at him.

PBTM 2

Alien-mum also has Doctor Zargle eyes. They're staring right at me over the shopping bag bulging with frozen chicken parts. Her eyes don't know anything about being chased; they only know about chasing. She huff-puffs at me and this helps turn her into a creature about one thousand times scarier than the shopping bag monster. This is when I suddenly realize I'm in a PBTM situation. This makes me say the first thing that comes into my head, which is, "You just flattened *Huckleberry Finn*."

This is a very stupid thing to say during a PBTM. But she doesn't even say anything. She just huff-puffs and stares at me without blinking. Right then the spoon-faced boy decides to touch the window with his little finger because the train has finally decided to move.

"Germs," she says without taking her eyes off me. She doesn't say it in a creepy voice but it feels really creepy. The effect of the word "germs" on the boy is a bit scary. He jumps like someone's jumped out on him in the dark. Then his coat falls open and I catch a big look at his name label. As soon as I see it, I instantly know why I feel so sorry for him. Because it says:

> My name is
> Tom Thumb.
> Pleased to meet you!

At first I worry about a sudden attack of the shoulder shakes. But it doesn't happen. No. Instead I feel slightly sick deep in my stomach like I've eaten something bad. I hide inside *Huckleberry Finn* after I've rescued it from certain death beneath the bulging bag of frozen chicken parts. But it's no good; the words have mysteriously turned into black squiggles again.

I sneak several looks at Tom Thumb and his mum because I can't seem to stop myself.

His mum and dad must have *really* hated him to call him that. Imagine the teacher reading your name out for the first time. Even the thought of it makes me feel sick. A name like that could make you stop liking anyone because you could never make yourself trust them.

Just think about it. Even if they weren't actually outside laughing at you, you'd always be worried they were secret-laughing instead.

The mum huff-puffs, and she huff-puffs, and she huff-puffs, "Germs!" again to poor Tom Thumb.

And again,

and again,

and again,

and again,

and again,

and again,

until I've completely lost count of all the agains and wish my dad was here to help me.

After about an hour and half I'm starting to worry about just how many germs there are in the world. I wouldn't mind but I'm not really sure what it is germs actually do or why they do it. I mean, I've enough to worry about without worrying about stuff I've never thought about before this exact second. My dad said if someone made a list of all the stuff I don't know about, it would need some sort of undiscovered astrophysics. To tell the truth I'm starting to think that finding things out isn't all it's cracked up to be. You need to be really careful about what you find out. Once you know something, it's there and that's that. You could say there's such a thing as forgetting but I don't think it makes it go away. I think it just becomes invisible inside your head and changes how you look at things.

When Alien-mum finally huff and puffs her way out to the toilet, I open my eyes and sit up.

"Is that really your mum?" I ask Tom Thumb.

He looks at me like I might be some new kind of germ for a moment. One found on frozen chicken parts. He then checks to make sure his mum isn't storming back. When he's sure she isn't, he nods at me. I point at his name tag. When he realizes I don't want to say it, his face softens a tiny little bit. Then he nods at me.

"Really?" I ask because I can't think of a way not to. The frozen-chicken germ look switches back on to his face again for a minute. He then searches around inside my face to see if I'm secret-laughing. When he seems sure I'm not, he leans forward and says, "There are over five hundred different kinds of bacteria living in your mouth right this second."

"Really?" I ask him because it definitely sounds like something new to worry about.

"Everyone's," he says. "Except mine."

"I'm glad it's not just me," I tell him.

Then we don't say anything for a while. Outside

the world goes scooting by the window as if it's in a big hurry to turn into the countryside.

"Are there a lot of germs about then?" I ask him because it's the only thing I can think of that isn't about his mad name. Tom Thumb gives me the frozen-chicken germ look again. I realize why he keeps looking at me that way. It's because *he's* so used to being looked at that way himself. Maybe he thinks that's how you're supposed to do it.

"Is your mum nuts?" I ask him. He stares his chased look out of his Doctor Zargle eyes but doesn't give me the frozen-chicken germ look. This is a relief. He then nods very, very slightly.

"Don't you like talking to people?" I ask him.

"There are over one billion germs," he says, "and they live all over you."

His saying I'm totally hopping with germs doesn't bother me. So I ask, "Are you covered in germs too?"

Tom Thumb shakes his head.

This makes me realize why I'm not bothered about germs hopping all over me. I'd rather just have them than not. Especially if the not part means you have to be as scared as Tom Thumb is all the time. Tom Thumb looks made up of scared the same way Lego buildings look made up of small plastic bricks.

Tom Thumb looks like the most scared person I've ever met. And he's not background scared, either. I know I'm running away but some bit of me thinks it might be running toward something. Don't ask me which bit because I don't know.

"I'm running away," I tell him. I don't know why; it just sort of pops out. He looks for his mum again then says, "Why?"

That's a very hard one. The reasons are like great, big dinosaurs stomping around inside me. So I say, "Because . . ." It's the only word that explains it all without using up the rest of our lives. It seems to be enough for him. At least, he gives me a new look like I mightn't be just another germ factory after all.

"Where are you going?" he asks. Then when I tell him I don't really know, he looks even more interested. "What does it feel like?" he asks.

"Dunno," I say, "I'm still sort of doing it."

"Oh," he says.

"There is a sort of bubbly feeling in my stomach all the time," I explain.

"That's just being scared," Tom Thumb says, sounding very sure. Then I explain about some of the other feelings like the going-on-holiday feeling and the being-on-a-big-train-alone feeling and the what's-going-to-happen-next feeling. When I finally go quiet again for a minute, Tom Thumb gets this terrible mixed-up look on his face and looks for his mum twice.

"I wish I could run away," he says, and spurts out a bubbly giggle. I think it is quite brave.

"What would be the first thing you'd do?" I ask

him. He gives me a look that says I'm really, really stupid. So I add, "After you change your name."

"Swim in the sea," he says. "I'd go right into the water with my clothes on. I wouldn't even care about the cold or pollution or mutated fish stocks or nuclear submarines or floating poo."

He then goes on and on for ages about all the things he'd do. And as he does so he slowly begins to stop looking chased and scared of everything. He starts to look like an ordinary kid. Like you or me.

Tom Thumb's runaway to-do list:

1. Change his name

2. Swim in the sea with his clothes on

3. Eat a lot of eggs

4. Stop washing forever or until he is caught

5. Climb Mount Everest

6. Go to the cinema

7. Live in a tent

8. Become a wrestler

9. Not know anything about germs

10. Get some mates

By the time he comes to the end of his list, Tom Thumb looks like he's moving even though he's sitting still. It's not being chased moving, either.

It makes me feel even more sorry for him.

After Finn our house became a bit like that. Every now and then you'd catch a little look underneath to what we used to be like. I mean before everyone had to start worrying about everyone else all the time. We used to have a really good laugh a lot of the time. Not all the time because that's just stupid, but a lot of the time. But the trouble was to have that little glimpse you had to forget about Finn. Then when you remembered about him again you'd feel a sudden drop inside you like you'd fallen off a cliff. Even if you'd forgotten him for only half a second it didn't matter. You still felt guilty because forgetting about him was such a relief. Then I began to think we were trying to forget him *because* it was a relief or we were supposed to or something like that.

I first noticed it one pizza and video night. On pizza night the phone got switched off and it was just us five. It always gave me that warm, tight feeling deep in my stomach, especially when the weather was bad outside. Pizza is always on a Friday except in school holidays. Anyway, this was the first pizza night since Finn and you could just tell everyone was pretending to make everyone else feel better, like it was business as usual. Then suddenly, for about one single nanosecond no one was pretending anything. It was during a funny bit of the video we were watching when everyone laughed at the same time, even Angela while Donut was nicking pizza crusts as usual. After that, pizza night stopped. No one said anything; it just ended like ending it *was* the most normal thing in the world.

But to be honest with you, inside I was really angry with Finn, as if it was his fault or something mad like that. It was *his* fault there were only four of us eating pizza and laughing with the rest of us. I know how terrible that sounds but it's true. And the funny thing is Finn loved a good laugh better than anyone else I know.

"You know a lot about germs," I point out just for something to say. "Are you ill or something?"

Tom Thumb seems to have secretly passed his being scared of everything over to me. Asking him about germs turns out to be a big mistake because he immediately lists a vast amount of diseases and illnesses there are to catch in the world. "My mum reads about them in a big secondhand medical book she found in a secondhand book shop." He makes it sound like he's explaining what a secondhand shop does. I'm a bit annoyed so I say, "Now that's a bit mad."

He looks at me funny, so I add, "Well, if she's *that* worried about diseases and illnesses you'd think she would have sprung for a new medical book."

Emergency bag of Cheesy Wotsits!

Because Tom Thumb's stopped looking out for his mum I've started.

"Is she always this long?" I ask him.

"Yes." He nods. He then goes on to explain how she always but always has to find the least dirty toilet on the train. When she does she cleans it. "That's why she carries such a big bag," he explains. "It's filled up with cleaning products and five pairs of rubber gloves."

When I ask him why five he says he doesn't know.

At this point I decide to take out my very last emergency bag of Cheesy Wotsits. I know I should try to hold on to them because I know the buffet car won't have any. But the truth is I could really do with them now. As soon as Tom Thumb spots them I realize it's a mistake.

He says, "Orange preservatives" in a very shaky voice. I open up the bag and offer him one. This also turns out to be a big mistake because he nicks the whole bag and proceeds to stuff them down his throat three at a time. He crunches and munches them like he hasn't eaten in about two months and Cheesy Wotsits are the best invention ever. I think about rescuing them for a second but finally don't bother. I don't bother even though I know the buffet car just has ready-salted crisps that don't taste of anything unless thick and crinkled are flavors.

It now feels like I've been on this train forever. There are these big, fat splats of rain getting smeared all over the window by the rushing wind. Their noise sounds like easy to break things getting broken. Now I'm scared to think about getting off at my station. Then I think, *Two hundred and seven miles*[1] but not normal miles. No. Two hundred and seven miles stretched out tight like an elastic band.

[1] That's how far I am from Holt Street.

Tom Thumb, Human Hoover!

I don't think I've ever liked anything as much as Tom Thumb likes my emergency packet of Cheesy Wotsits. I mean, he likes them so much it's a bit scary. I get the feeling he's trying to eat up everything he's ever missed. But not even just that, no, Tom Thumb wants to eat every single thing he's going to miss some other time like next week or the week after that.

As I watch, he rips the empty bag open and spreads it out flat on the table. He does it really carefully, pinning the edges with two orange index fingers. He then does something a bit mad. He starts to lick up every single bit of orange dust he can find. He uses the very, very tip of his tongue. At first his tongue darts out like a snake, then he begins to do it in exact, straight lines. He pauses every few seconds to make sure he hasn't missed one. Then when he spots one teeny-tiny bit of Wotsit has tried to escape by hiding on the tip of his nose, his tongue snakes out and gets it. Tom Thumb is only the second person I know who can touch his nose with the tip of his tongue. The other boy is Bob Cox. He would do it in the playground at break time. You had to queue up and pay him with sweets or crisps.

By the time Tom Thumb is finished, the Cheesy Wotsit bag is completely clean. He then hunts around the tabletop with a wet finger and dabs up any strays. He then starts to work on his fingers and thumbs like maybe he's decided to eat himself out of existence. In about five seconds the bag and the table and himself are as clean as one of his mum's toilets. I want to give him a clap just like he's a magician who's finished a bit of sword swallowing.

TOM THUMB, HUMAN HOOVER!

The Alien-mum comes trundling back down the aisle from the cleanest toilet on the train. I think about asking her what toilet it is. *I'm* now really worried about germs.

As soon as she sits down, Tom Thumb puts on his Doctor Zargle head again.

And she knows.

I can tell by the way she looks around the table. Her eyes glare over the bulging shopping bags. I hide behind *Huckleberry Finn* but keep on watching her. I have the terrible feeling she somehow knows all about the emergency bag of Cheesy Wotsits.

"He made me," Tom Thumb says, pointing a Cheesy Wotsit finger at me as if he's worried Alien-mum will think he means someone else. And I can't believe the evil little git has done it. I mean, he didn't even wait to be asked. Alien-mum gives me a look as if she could squish me like a tiny insect and the only thing stopping her is all the witnesses.

"Allergic," she says to me. I decide to drop him in it to return the favor.

"I only offered him one and he scoffed the lot," I explain to her. Don't get me wrong, I'm not usually the kind of person who daubs people in, but I think you'll agree Tom Thumb deserves it. "And it was my emergency bag of Cheesy Wotsits."

"Highly allergic," she says in a voice falling like concrete blocks.

Anyway, five minutes later I've had enough of being glared at like I'm some kind of disease so I decide to pretend I'm asleep. I start listening to the creaking and whooshing of the train slipping through the afternoon and soon I'm really sleeping.

I have this swimming dream about Finn and me. We're in the river and he's beating me in a race. He's beating me because I've forgotten how to swim and the water is icy cold. He shouts my name and his voice sounds whisper close even though he's far away. The last thing I remember is his head bobbing up and down like an otter's. Then it disappears.

Growl

The train wakes me up by stopping. I peep first but Tom Thumb and his alien-mum have gone along with their shopping. In fact, when I look around I see I'm the only person left in the whole carriage. Outside it's evening and a bit rainy and this is where I need to get off the train. As I step down to the platform I try hard not to be glad Tom Thumb is called Tom Thumb.

It doesn't work.

I close the door and the conductor looks at me for a second before blowing his whistle and climbing back onto the train. The noise of the engine is deafening when the train goes but the silence it leaves behind seems very deep and permanent and worse. The station has a dark, abandoned look about it. It makes me feel very far from home. The wind is making a low whining sound and pushing the tiny pinpricks of cold rain under the overhanging platform roof to get me. A little white dog comes along to growl at me when I try to pet it. Then it leaves and I follow it out of the station.

When I'm outside the station I notice it, the smell of the sea.

Ha-ha-ha

The island isn't really an island. That is, not all the time. When the tide goes out it's joined to the land. When the tide's out it looks a bit like a giant hand. As soon as I walk down the hill from the station past the houses, I notice the tide is still out so I can cross to it. I think, *Now what?* I think this for a number of reasons. It's cold and shivery and rainy. There's loads of heavy-looking clouds hanging over me like wet sponges. The sea is gray and annoyed and the waves are making a hissing, whooshing noise. But the worst thing is a big flock of gulls who are laughing very loudly at me. They stop for a minute or so, then one flaps its wings and starts them all off again. And it's not a very friendly laugh. No. It's the laugh some kids use in school to let you know they're glad you've hurt yourself.

Somehow I thought that standing here on this beach where we were really happy as a family would change how I feel about things. But it hasn't, apart from making me feel a bit worse, actually.

I walk along the curve of the inlet toward the rocks. I go to the exact spot where Finn and me spotted a family of sea otters fishing. I remember their five little heads bobbing up and down with the dark blue waves like candy. The falling mist has hidden most of the rocks and I can only hear the sea. And to top it all off the wind is now doing a very bad impression of a ghost in my ear. But that remembered day is kind of shining inside me. It must be because I've had so much time to polish it up by thinking about it over and over. Not speaking for six weeks gives you loads of time to do just that. But even though I'm standing here right this second it doesn't seem like somewhere I know. The memory of it inside my head seems a lot more real to me. It's not cold and wet and howling.

My mum and dad and Angela and Finn and me are standing on the rocks watching the slick candy-headed otters bobbing up and down, bobbing up and down.

And now, just this very second I suddenly feel really close to them. We had a brilliant laugh here in a way that can't ever happen again. And knowing even that doesn't hurt the way you'd think it should. And before you say anything about me being heartless, well, it's not like that one little bit. It does hurt but it also feels good at the same time. Because it *did* happen and no matter what, it will go on having happened forever and ever.

End of story.

Spooky

I look up at the houses perched above this tiny inlet floating in the misty rain. The lights are flickering on one by one as the darkness comes down. I'm looking for the holiday house we stayed in but I can't spot it. The mist and the rain are helping the evening to hide it from me. Even though I can't see the sea, it has filled up the air with stinging salt spray by banging itself against the rocks. Now the rain is getting heavier. Its big fat splats sound like sausages sizzling.

There is definitely a storm coming.

I really need to find somewhere to spend the night. I've remembered an old boathouse along the shore behind the trees. Finn and me found it when we were spotting sea otters early one morning. We begged Mum and Dad to let us sleep over in it and were very shocked when they said yes. It was one of the best nights ever even though it was a bit spooky. We didn't sleep much. We just lay in our sleeping bags with our flashlights and told ghost stories.

I try very hard not to remember any of the stories as I hurry down the beach. I can't stop myself from remembering that there were a lot of maniacs because we were really into horror films at the time. The wind is making everything move in big, mad swirls as it howls along the beach. It keeps shoving and tugging at me and throwing salt spray in my eyes.

I trip over an invisible stump put there by the night and go headfirst into a shallow pool of freezing seawater. I'm soaked through and quivering like a jelly. I can't see because the spray is stinging my eyes out. I can't hear a thing except for the wind roaring around like a train. I suddenly get a feeling of just how big all of this is.

I want to be home. I want to be lying in my bunk

bed sniggering because Finn is wriggling around in the bunk above farting out a song and sniggering, too. The time I'm thinking of must be a pizza and video night because his bottom always spoke Italian after pizza. I want it so much it stings like a paper cut on my thumb. Then the wind blows right up my nose and makes me snort like a pig.

This is when I finally start to cry.

It pops in me like a bubble right here in the middle of this stupid storm. It comes gushing out of me in a way I couldn't stop even if I wanted to. I'm just too cold and wet and blind and deaf to manage it.

What comes pouring out is:

Finn

and that stupid stuffed otter,

and not saying one single word for six weeks exactly,

and Angela and the big slide,

and my mum not knowing what a real mum should look like,

and my dad counting and counting and counting
because *he* can't think what else to do,

and being cold and wet and deaf and blind and
sitting in this tidal pool and being lost in this
storm,

and having a numb bum right this second.

It's all come howling out of me to the very last
drop. And just as there seems to be nothing left, I
remember Tom Thumb ate my bag of emergency
Wotsits.

Remembering this doesn't help one tiny little bit.

Now I'm really, really scared, and I know I'm
supposed to deserve all of it. But I don't think
there's a rule written down somewhere that says I
have to like it and not have a big bloody moan
about it.

Brilliant idea!

Then in the middle of all this two good things happen. The first is I notice my bag is still dry because it's dangling from my hand which is held high in the air. This means *Huckleberry Finn* and the rest of my stuff didn't join me for a swim. The second good thing is this big, massive boom of lightning. It ignites the whole night and almost causes a PBTM before showing me the shape of the storm and the old boathouse. The storm is all slants and swirls and the shadow of the boathouse is a solid, black square that makes me feel better for a moment. The lightning also shows me it was the rotted hull of an old boat that sent me flying.

I quickly get to my feet and slouch/squelch over to the boathouse. Even above the storm I can hear it creaking and groaning like it's hurt and there's no one to help it but me. But once I get the door open, I stop for a moment. The open door makes the inside look like a big, black throat with a bad breath problem. I mean, even in the wind you can tell if it smelled any fishier it would live in the sea.

I hold my breath and go in.

I stumble around in the dark for about five years before I remember the box of matches in my bag. The rumbling thunder sounds like someone moving big heavy wardrobes about next door even though there isn't a next door. Everything is creaking and stretching like someone breathing into a paper bag to stop being sick. The boathouse sounds like it's going to collapse at any second. And in between gusts there's the constant roar of the sea.

So,

I'm blind,

I'm wet,

I'm shivering like a dog,

I'm scared of this whole place flattening me,

I'm scared of being struck by lightning,

I'm scared of being washed away by the sea.

What a brilliant idea it was to come here.

Doing

@

The smell of fish is so bad it's managed to get my mind off Cheesy Wotsits. Well, at least I'm out of the storm. I strike a match and the light makes the storm take a step back for a moment. The shadows flicker around me like bats as I check the floor. There's enough lumps of rotted wood and old rope to keep a fire going for a while. Then the match goes out. After I've burned my fingers three times, I grope around in the darkness for fuel. When I've got enough, I light a little fire.

I should be good at lighting fires because Dad and Finn and me used to go camping a lot together. And to be honest that's how I'm getting through this right now. I'm pretending I'm on a camping trip and Dad and Finn are off fishing. I can almost hear them returning to wind me up because I've made such a pig's ear out of this little fire of mine.

It takes ages to get it going properly because bits of storm come through the creaking walls to blow it out on me. I'm now shivering so much I'm worried it might be possible to shake something important loose inside me. After about an hour or so the fire is warm enough to make steam rise from my wet clothes. Above the bright flames, the drafts are pushing the smoke into swirls near the ceiling. It's making me cough a bit but I sort of lie on the sandy ground and watch them, hoping they don't turn into otters or anything too mad like that.

And now that I've stopped, I realize all the time I've been doing stuff I wasn't thinking about things. I mean, I was scared outside and all but it was only about being caught in the storm right there that moment. And just now finding fuel and building my little fire was only about drying my clothes and not being cold. It felt like just doing something that simple had its own reasons and that was that. Doing is just the exact second you do it. After that it's something else. Another thing I have to admit is underneath all the scariness I'm having a bit of a laugh. Underneath is an excited tingly feeling. I'm sorry if I'm not supposed to feel it but I do. You can't help how you feel about things. Can you?

The tingly feeling doesn't belong to now; it belongs to that time when I stayed here for the night with Finn. It was even raining then, too, but not as heavy.

Some of the things we said to each other

Finn farted and even though it was muffled by his *Batman* sleeping bag you could still hear it. You could hear it above the rain and wind outside.

"Watch out for low-flying ducks," he shouted.

"Was that a real one?" I asked, even though it sounded real and he was a champion farter.

"Yeah," he said, straining to do another one.

"No way."

"Yes it was."

"Hand under your arm," I said.

"Was," he said, then added, "You'll smell it in a minute."

We both laughed a lot after that until I smelt it and started gagging. It reminded me of the ones Old Grundy was always dropping. After I'd stopped choking I asked him, "Do you think there's really real maniacs running about?"

I'd been thinking about a horror film we'd seen around at Bod's party because his mum and dad don't care what he's seen.

"Tony Rumsey's a maniac," Finn said. Which was true.

"Yeah and so're all his mates," I said. "But that's not the sort of maniac I mean."

"What do you mean?"

"I mean one *here*."

I was instantly spooked and sort of wriggled down in my *Spider-Man* sleeping bag.

"Do you think maniacs come on holiday?" Finn whispered. I knew he was winding me up *because* he was spooked, too.

"Yeah," I said.

Then we were quiet for a while and listened to the dry rain.

Finally I said I didn't think they really went on holiday. "At least they don't in films," I explained.

"Maniacs always get you in places like this," Finn croaked in a scary voice.

"That means they'll get you, too," I said. "What if he only comes after me because he thinks I'm you?"

"Shut up," Finn said.

We were both quiet for a moment after that.

I started thinking about what I'd say to a maniac if he did turn up. I don't think he'd leave you alone for a Mars bar and a packet of Cheesy Wotsits.

"What kind of crisps do you think one would like?" I whispered.

Finn was quiet for a while, then he said, "Pickled Onion, Monster Munch" in a growling maniac voice.

Later as we were drifting off to sleep, I remember he asked me what I wanted to be when I grew up.

I said, "A mountain climber."

But when I asked him the same question he didn't answer because he'd fallen asleep.

I drift off now as the wind and the rain tear the world to pieces and the sound of them chases me into my sleep.

Boom!

Suddenly I wake up and for a moment I don't know where I am. The storm has faded to a slow sizzle of rain on the roof and the fire has burned down to a glow. I immediately build it up again and am enjoying the fresh heat when I think I hear something. I listen so hard my ears start to buzz but there's nothing but the rain. Then I hear it again. It sounds like someone moving around just outside the boathouse. It must have been the noise that woke me up. Realizing this sends shivery ripples of fear all through me.

Whoever it is must know I'm here because of the firelight.

Now I'm wondering who would be out in a storm in the middle of the night. Thinking this doesn't help me feel any better. As I take out my

Swiss Army knife[1], my head is filling with all the horror stories we made up about this place last year. The knife seems very small in the firelight. Then it all goes quiet again for a minute and I get the creeping feeling that I'm being watched. It wouldn't be hard with the walls having more holes than a string vest.

Now I'm sure I can hear someone breathing.

Thinking about this is making my bottom go ten p/five p at a mile a minute. I'm more scared now than the time Bobby Thompson threatened to stuff my head down the toilet at school. And it hadn't even been flushed. Finn saved me by booting him really hard on the shin. Then we both jumped on him and put *his* head down the toilet.

I'm having a hard time stopping myself having a spot of (secret) shoulder-shake laughing when the movement starts up again. It's moving along the boathouse toward the front. I stand up and sneak toward the door. I'm looking for something to put

---

[1] Granddad bought Finn and me one each for our birthday.

against it to stop the creeper from getting in. I trip over a rope and go flying. And worst of all I let go of my Swiss Army knife. As I'm groping around for it I remember that the door opens out *because* it's a boathouse after all. My head is now completely filled up with horror stories where I'm the hero who has something depressing happen to him. I'm so scared now I'm shaking like Donut when he knows he's going to the vet. Even when I find my Swiss Army knife, it doesn't stop. I crawl to the door and press my ear against it.

Suddenly there's a booming knock on the door. *Boom! Boom!* It rattles the rusty hinges and makes me jump back and almost land in the fire. I freeze while my heart beats like mad. There's about a pint of spit suddenly dumped into my mouth.

Then the door starts to open.

There's this man standing in the doorway. I can't see his face because he has the hood of his windcheater pulled up. He's holding up an old lamp.

Behind him the rain is sizzling down like a shower curtain. The man is wet and slick as if he's made out of this stormy night. Nothing happens for a minute and we just sort of stare at each other.

"Are you okay?" the man asks.

I'm so nervous I fart.

"I'll take that as a yes," he says, and then he just closes the door.

Part Two

Doing

Weeing

When I finally wake up it's because I'm really bursting for a wee. As soon as I open my eyes, I notice a spider looking at me from a lump of wood. I normally don't mind spiders but this one is big enough to nick my sneakers if I'm not careful.

I start thinking about the storm man and wonder what he thought about me letting one go because I was so scared. Then I notice them— millions of beams of light crisscrossing in the darkness. They must be coming through from pinprick holes in the walls and the ceiling. When I check my clothes, I find they're all dry except for my socks and one trainer. My hoody has patches of dried salt all over the arms where I landed headfirst in the tidal pool. The material smells like you think chemicals should. When I finally push open the door, my eyes are stung by a big burst of morning light. I have to blink for ages before the sparkles go away.

There's a breeze coming in from the sea which is about forty feet away. I place my wet trainer and socks in a patch of sunlight to dry, then go and explore the beach.

The storm has littered the beach with things. There's lots of wood which is good news for me. There is also a red shed door with the hinges still attached. And there's a No Entry sign and the bottom half of a rocking horse and a toilet seat. Scattered here and there are what look like a lot of rubber Frisbees, but they turn out to be flattened jellyfish. There are even a couple of my footprints left from where I crossed over the beach. I look at the tide flowing and it's hard to imagine I walked on the sand underneath where fish are swimming. I climb over it all and go toward the sea. I look across to the other shore and wonder if there's footprints there, too. It looks to be about fifty feet away but I could be wrong. Everything feels close and faraway at the same time. When I look up and hide my eyes from the sun, the blue sky is filled with distant clouds being torn into different shapes by the wind.

I roll up my trouser legs and let the seawater shock me and numb my feet. My feet sink into the gritty wet sand so I squeeze it between my toes. Then I have a wee. A wee in the sea when you're standing in it is one of the best things in the world you can do. But as I do it I suddenly remember doing it with Finn over by the rocks. How I'm remembering him now makes it like he's almost here right beside me having a steamy sword fight. This close feeling doesn't make me feel at all bad. Truth is, I'm glad to be feeling it.

It was my dad who advised us to try weeing in the sea. And we did once we worked out he wasn't winding us up. He also said we should try to do it as much as possible before we hit thirteen. He said after that it wasn't the same and anyway people become less forgiving as you get older.

Nothing to do with me

After I've finished my wee I go over to a big rock and sit on it for a while. The gulls are calling to each other like they're looking for something funny to laugh at. But today it isn't me.

And as I sit here looking and just breathing in and out, everything inside me begins to fade into the background. It doesn't go away. I mean, I know it'll never do that. It just feels like the volume has been turned down for a while or I'm on a break from it. I start to think about my mum and my dad and my sister and it feels like they're here with me a little bit. So putting that brick with three holes in it through Old Grundy's window and flattening his stupid stuffed otter has nothing to do with me. It feels like someone else did it and just told me about it after.

The last big thing we all did together (part one)

I go down to the water's edge again. I just stand looking at the sea and rubbing the sand between my toes. I then crouch down and push my hands down into the sand. It's warm on top but cold underneath. All the tiny little grains between my fingers suddenly make everything jump straight at me.

I think this is the exact spot we built the sand castle the day before our holiday ended. It gives me a light feeling for a second when I realize it was the very last big thing we did all together.

A rubbish sand castle.

But it was a really big rubbish sand castle.

We were just glad to be out because it was what my mum calls a windcheater sort of holiday. We'd spent the whole time being driven all over the place and being made to learn things in museums because it wouldn't stop raining. It was almost as bad as school.

Anyway the rain suddenly stopped so we all sprinted down to this beach with our buckets and spades and inflatable holiday stuff before it changed its mind again.

In less than one minute we felt like we owned this beach and that we always had and always would. Over there, Mum and Dad were instantly lying in the sun tent reading while Donut kept on dashing down to bark at the sea before dashing back up to pant in the shade. Finn and me were over at those rocks on Angela patrol. She was where I am now; we could see her in her mad red-and-white-spotted swimming suit and her brown monkey hat. Finn and me were having a wee sword fight because we were bored watching Angela putting shells from her blue plastic bucket onto a small sand castle she'd just made.

"Know Airplane Kev?" Finn asked me.

"What about him?" I asked.

"He's a big rubbish-looking bouncy castle."

Then we both started laughing because it was such a stupid thing to say. But what we were really laughing about was something Airplane Kev had said to us just before we went on holiday. Bod had gotten him to ask us if our willies were exactly the same as well.

How stupid is that?

Anyway we told him no because we only had one willy that we had to share between us. And if one of us needed to go, even if it was really badly, and it wasn't your turn, well, you'd just have to wait until it was.

The worst thing was you could actually see him almost believing it. So that's what we were laughing about.

Then we stopped talking because I weed on Finn's foot and he weed on mine. Then we both weed on each other but not for very long because we'd run out. Then Finn said, "C'mon, we'll help her build one," and he ran before I answered because he knew I'd come.

So I did.

The last big thing we all did together (part two)

The sand castle was more of a sand lump with some shells stuck on it because that's all a little kid like Angela could do.

Finn was already pretending it was good when I got there so I pretended, too. She must've known it was rubbish because when we went on about how good it was, she gave us a really dirty look to make us stop. She's really clever even though she's deaf. Then I signed something about helping her and Finn did the same.

Angela gave us this serious look for a moment, then signed, *Get lost.*

She must've thought we were still winding her up. We were but only a tiny little bit, maybe 10 percent or something like that.

It'll be massive, I signed and Finn added, *If we do it together.*

Angela thought about it for a bit longer, then she signed, *It's still my sand castle no matter what.*

So Finn and me nodded; Angela nodded, too.

We started by digging a big circle down to where the sand was wet. We dug toward each other with our hands because Angela wouldn't loan us her spade because we'd wound her up. Donut came down to bark at the sea again but decided to dig a hole instead when he saw us. It wasn't much help because he showered us with wet sand. We didn't mind because he needed the exercise. Donut had been put on a diet since he's been fixed.

Even though Donut was really thick from banging his head into things all the time, he gave us a good idea for piling sand. We went inside the circle we'd finished and began to doggie pile sand inside. Angela was laughing because we looked so stupid. When she'd finished she went off along the shore for a bit to find some more shells to put in her blue plastic bucket.

After a couple of minutes our dad had to come

down because Finn and me were now pelting each other with wet sand. Then we pelted Donut who'd started it.

"Knock it off you two," my dad said.

I said, "Danny started it."

And he said, "No, Finn started it."

My dad just stared at us with this bored look on his face for a second, then said, "I don't care who started it because I just finished it."

His voice sounded like it could've gone either way so we stopped.

"You'll have someone's eye out carrying on like that," Mum shouted down from the sun tent. Then she said, "Oh and while you halfwits are busy blinding each other I can see Angela is too near the water."

Mum can be like that sometimes.

My dad went off to rescue her so we went back to piling sand.

The last big thing we all did together (part three)

When he came back my dad just dropped to his knees and started digging. His big hands were just like Granddad's. I really liked watching them shovel up the sand. When I looked at Finn, I could see he was thinking the same thing. It was like they belonged to this big shoveling-dad machine we couldn't keep up with. I really wanted my hands to be like his when I grew up but I didn't want to be bald.

Then Finn nodded and started grinning. I looked and saw my dad's big bald head was turning as red as a traffic signal in the sun. We both did some secret shoulder-shake laughter for a few moments.

"Baldness is hereditary, you know," Dad said without looking up.

"That's okay, we don't know what 'hereditary' means, Dad," Finn said.

My dad started grinning and said, "You'll find out."

We worked on that sand castle for most of the day. Mum even lent a hand. When she and Angela came down they spent ages covering the sand castle in the shells they'd collected. There was even a lot left over so we helped Angela write her name in shells in the sand. She grinned so much I thought the top of her head would fall off.

The sun was setting and the sand castle was casting a big, long shadow. We kept looking over our shoulders at it even though we knew it wasn't brilliant and wouldn't win any prizes unless they have one for being big and rubbish. It was wonky at the top and the tide had washed away part of the moat. We couldn't care less because we'd had such a good laugh building it.

Now I look down at the sand in my hands and I

catch myself thinking, *Is this a bit of it or is this?* even though I know it's impossible to know. Then I make myself stop and stand up again. I brush the sand away and as I do I feel this big bubble of being lost and alone come rising up inside me. It makes me feel a bit sick.

The sand castle won't come back even if I look forever. Besides, that all belongs to before. And thinking about it just makes me miss it more.

And it's not coming back.

None of it.

Never.

To do

Now as I walk toward the boathouse all the to-do stuff comes whizzing back to me. Stuff like I'm hungry and I need some water and I'm nearly out of matches. It pushes everything about sand castles and missing things out of my head. Then I notice the door of the boathouse is closed.

It's closed even though I remember leaving it open.

PBTM Three

As I get closer my legs start going a bit wobbly and I feel a PBTM is happening. I can't see anyone hovering about but that doesn't mean anything. They could be hiding. Next I start wondering who *they* are. It could be the police but it's more likely to be the storm man. What if he has come back? What if he's now hiding inside the boathouse, *his* boathouse and is ready to get me? I finally stop behind a rock covered in seaweed. I need to think about what to do next.

The boathouse is the only shelter I know of on the island. I think about crossing to the mainland and going up the hill to find an empty holiday home to stay in. But the tide is in and I'd rather not add breaking and entering to the crime of stuffed otter flattening right now. I also remember I've left all my things in the boathouse and I'll feel really stupid running around in my bare feet. Then I have the feeling I'm being watched.

I decide to sneak around the back of the boathouse through the trees. I need to have a look and make sure it wasn't the wind that shoved the door shut again.

It takes me ages to reach the trees because I have to climb over some sharp rocks. When I find the back of the boathouse, I move along the wall the storm man came by with his old lamp shining last night. I come to the end of the wall and I wait for a few moments listening. I've just about convinced myself that it was the wind after all when I notice the toe of a sneaker poking out. I freeze but my stomach does a mad jump and my heart starts running. Then I realize it's one of mine. After that it's shoulder shake, shoulder shake, shoulder shake and hiss-hiss-hiss for about ten minutes until it gets too stupid. So I step out and if someone's going to get me then I'll come quietly.

There's no one there.

There's no one there but it still wasn't the wind that shoved the boathouse door closed. My sneakers have been placed together. They've been placed together the same way my mum and dad do when they've tidied our room up. Then I notice something else.

Doing (part two)

◎

Someone has placed a folded sleeping bag on the sand beside my sneakers. I approach it slowly, half expecting a policeman to leap out from under it because they've dug a tunnel. A bit mad, I know, but I'm feeling a bit mad at the moment. The sleeping bag is covered in millions of tiny spots. At first I think it's just a naff pattern but it turns out to be a lot of different-colored spots and splats of paint. When I touch it no alarm bells go off, the police don't jump up, and the storm man doesn't leap out of the boathouse in his soaking windcheater. And to tell the truth, after all that sneaking and listening and hurting my feet, I'm a bit disappointed.

Beneath the paint-spotted sleeping bag I find a big bottle of water, a small flashlight, two tracker bars[1], an apple, and a bag of crisps.[2] The bottle of water

---

[1] I normally don't like tracker bars.
[2] Not Cheesy Wotsits

and the flashlight have tiny flecks of paint all over them, too. I pull open the boathouse door and look in. I'm still being careful but it's more like a game now. The sun paints a big yellow rectangle on the darkness of the boathouse floor. It's filled up with floating dust motes and trailing cobwebs. The floor's still littered with wood and snakes of rope. My little fire has a tiny trickle of white smoke hovering about it that looks a bit sad and left behind.

I decide to do a tidy up.

It takes ages to clear the floor and by the time I finish I'm covered in sweat. I stack the wood at the back of the boathouse and drag the rope outside. I then build the fire nearer the door and put a circle of stones around it. I unroll the paint-spotted sleeping bag between the fire and the door. I put the apple, the bottle of water, the crisps, and the tracker bars and the flashlight on a flat wall support that does as a shelf. The last thing I do is go out and gather a lot of sticks and twigs, then build the fire without lighting it. Hopefully they won't smoke too much because of the damp. I don't bother about the cobwebs because I don't want anything with more legs than me dropping down on my head.

Even though I find myself crouching each time I move around, the place isn't too bad. Now the ground has been cleared, the sand is soft and powdery. I sit on the sleeping bag and sort of enjoy what I've done. I bet my mum would need a long lie down if she could see it. I then unpack my bag.

I dig out:

1. two T-shirts

2. two pairs of pants

3. some toilet paper[1]

4. *Huckleberry Finn*

5. the last of my matches[2]

6. my toothpaste and toothbrush

7. my windcheater[3]

---

[1] Because you never know.
[2] Four
[3] I'd forgotten I'd packed it.

Sadly there isn't one single Cheesy Wotsit in sight. I think about Tom Thumb for a second but thoughts about him don't seem to belong here. I feel like I'm sitting inside all these tiny little bits of doing. Not tangled up but snug like a finger in a glove. And this tiny little bit of thinking about things feels like just the right amount of thinking to do. So I stop right there.

Skimming

◎

The good thing about skimming stones is you don't have to think about it if you don't want to. It's dead easy to disappear into it all. It doesn't need to have any words attached to it.

Anyway I'm collecting skimming stones when I suddenly start thinking about the Great Wall of China. I'm thinking about it because it's the only thing people have done that you can see from outer space. Then because it seems to be becoming a day about stones, I feel that I should leave something made of stones behind. A something to show I've been here at this moment.

I skim stones for a bit[1] while I try to think about what to make. It needs to be something good but right this moment I can't think about anything except skimming stones. Now it needs

---

[1] The best is six skims before the plop.

to be really good because *wanting* to do it has suddenly become *having* to do it. I immediately decide it doesn't need to be visible from space. No. It just needs to be visible to me.

Whispers

Sitting here on this rock that looks like a big, pointing toe, I'm being warmed up by the early evening sun. I keep catching myself looking out for that family of otters. It's a stupid thing to do because they're probably long gone. Sea otters are different from river otters. For a start, they're not nocturnal and don't have to sneak around all over the place. River otters are really hard to see even though they tend to stick to a part of river they like. That's because people used to wear them or stuff them or whatever. This meant the otter had to be dead first, of course. So like badgers they probably worked out it's safer at night because people aren't around much then.

River otters are also quiet as whispers. Sea otters couldn't give a monkey's. That's because there isn't much around that can catch them. When they leg it, sea otters have somewhere to leg it to. That wouldn't be so bad, I mean, no matter how scary things got you could just grab your little otter family and run for it any time you had to.

I watch the waves froth and bubble on the sand for a bit because it makes me feel quiet. When I look up, I notice the mainland is more brown than green now and looks farther away than ever.

I don't mind.

Big Stones

But there don't seem to be very many big stones lying around. It's not that sort of beach. Then I get lucky when I search toward the trees. There's thousands of old, ruined bricks lying all over the place. Enough for my dad to build one hundred shaky sheds if he wanted to. Some even have three holes. This gives me a small laugh even though I'm slightly disappointed. When I thought of the idea, the stones were real ones, not bricks. But I suppose it doesn't matter.

Building (two)

When I've gone and got my bottle of water, I make a first big pile of bricks where I find them. I allow myself a mouthful of water every fifty bricks or so. When the pile has about five hundred bricks, I then start on another about halfway to the place I've chosen. I carry the bricks in stacks of four because three wasn't enough and five made me trip and land on my head.

It takes at least two hours to do it and by the time I'm finished I'm wrecked. I decide to stop for a while when I crush two fingernails between some bricks. I sit on the pile and allow myself a long drink of water. There's about half of the bottle left. I have a laugh for a moment looking through it at the sea and seeing it covered in paint splats. My T-shirt is filthy and soaked through with sweat. Then

I notice my belly has more red stripes on it than a football jersey. My arms are covered in nicks and scratches. My eyes are stinging and my body feels gritty and slippery at the same time. I've disappeared so far into making piles of bricks that everything else feels hazy in the same way other peoples' stories are hazy. I look at my hands and I count about five blisters, six small cuts, and one big cut that's smeared my fingers with blood. A hazy thing I remember: my granddad Joe telling me how some workmen used to wee on their hands to make them tough. I think I'd rather have the blisters.

Plop

Finally I decide to have a swim in the sea then dry myself off with my hoody afterward. As I walk to the edge of the water, I notice the sun is setting. I've been stacking bricks all afternoon. I am also starting to shiver because the sweat is drying on my skin. My hands feel like lead copies of real hands. The water is freezing and makes my head feel sort of numb and far away. I go back to the boathouse for something to eat and maybe light my fire because I'm shivering and need a dry T-shirt.

I drag the spotty sleeping bag to the entrance of the boathouse. I'm too tired to do anything but watch the sunset. The tide has snuck in again to make a big black space between me and the mainland. For a little while I become just this scared kid who doesn't know what to do next. Panic begins to bubble around inside me. I start thinking that being here is just my way of kicking a fence with a big dog behind it. Then the stars come out and I can't believe how clear they are. The breeze has scrubbed the clouds away. The stars feel very close.

The panic pours out of me leaving my head empty but clear. I tug the spotty sleeping bag up around my chin. Now I feel suddenly completely glad to be here, to be shivering inside this old sleeping bag. I know I can disappear into it like skimming stones or stacking bricks. And if I did I wouldn't have to remember anything ever again ever. I could be here shivering inside this spotty old sleeping bag because it doesn't matter. Because inside it is me and not him. I could take his place and it would go on being okay because somehow he would know how to stop my dad counting everything because he has to, and my mum worrying about what a good mum is because she has to, and he'd tug Angela out from under everything that's about to flatten her right at the last second. And all this would happen and keep on happening because I'm sitting shivering inside this old spotty sleeping bag dreaming the stars forever.

All these mad thoughts come skimming and plopping through me. Skimming things always seem to know where they're going right up to the second they go *plop*.

Now I know I must be asleep because my dad is talking to me. His voice comes drifting to me across the bay but it's close and warm. He's counting the stars with his finger. But that's okay because it's not his panicked counting. No. It's before and he's with Finn and me and we're all lying on the beach together. Dad's making us count the stars with our fingers so we know how impossible it is to do. Now he's explaining all the things that had to happen and go on happening just so we can be lucky enough to do something as simple as counting stars with our fingers. He starts with the creation of the universe and ends with his meeting our mum. It seems like an awful lot of things. Then I ask him if this is before what happened to Finn and he says no, it's after. He then says he's bored with us pretending.

Then I ask him about Finn and he explains that he was left at the train station by mistake. Finn starts going hiss-hiss-hiss and I realize it's because Dad's bald head looks like the moon. So I join in. And even though we don't tell Dad, I get the feeling he knows.

The sunlight wakes me up. The boathouse is exactly like I left it except that there's another bottle of water that wasn't there last night. There's also a covered plate that smells like curry and a piece of paper flapping like a bird's wing under a stone. The note has some paint specks on it and it says:

Come and say hello

Because I'm so hungry I eat the curry cold with my fingers. I don't even stop to worry if it's poison. I'm glad of this because it might mean I'm stopping being as mad as I've been for the last few weeks. For a while after Finn I stopped eating as well as speaking. To tell the truth I started thinking everyone was trying to poison me. Sitting here now with curry on my fingers, I can't believe how mad it was to think that. When I've finished, I notice the spoon he left.

I wash my hands in the sea. Then I start piling bricks again almost at once. Now I take my time and only carry three bricks at a go. I also wrap them in my hoody so my belly won't get nipped or my fingers cut anymore than they are already. I still don't think about what all these bricks are going to be when I've finished. And to tell the truth, I don't even know when I'll have piled enough. What I do know is I *have* to keep piling them, no matter what.

When I've finished work for the morning I have a swim to clean up. It doesn't last long because I'm worried about some fish coming along and nibbling my willy; besides, the water is freezing. I then wash out my hoody and stretch it on a rock to dry. I'm hoping it doesn't rain and the gulls don't use it for target practice.

The last thing I do is wash the storm man's bowl and spoon even though I didn't use it and the empty water bottle. I've decided to bring them all back.

The storm man

It's not hard to find where he's living. I just follow the smell of woodsmoke and curry. Then I notice a thin, curly, chip-shaped stream of smoke rising above the trees behind the boathouse on the opposite shore facing the open sea. There's also the sound of music. I know it's Bob Marley because my mum and dad play him a lot. I don't mind him but Finn hated him. I don't think Angela cares. Anyway, it sort of boom-boom-booms through the trees like someone calling me. I start feeling a bit nervous about seeing him. I mean, I don't even know what he looks like or why he gave me all that stuff or even why he hasn't booted me off the island or anything. I know he wouldn't have left the paint-spotted sleeping bag or the food and water for that matter if he was going to. All this thinking makes me feel confused and jumpy so I try to think about something else.

I can't.

It's tough going because the trees are so dense and there is a steep sort of rise. But once I start down the other side, it gets easier. His place is in a glade where the hill dips down like a big hole. I can see the open sea but the breeze can't get you here. The trees stop it. The place is a bit like a permanent campsite. But there are different-sized flower pots everywhere I look. They form a sort of border around his camp. The whole place is splashed with color. There are twisted lumps of driftwood everywhere. The music is coming from a bright orange camper van. He must have driven it across at low tide. There's a green tent attached to it by the open sliding door. The fire is smoldering near it. It's held in by a rough circle of bricks with a table and two chairs underneath. As I walk toward the music, I notice a little stream with a path worn beside it disappearing around the right of the camper van toward the sound of the sea.

There's no sign of anyone.

I think about calling out but somehow it feels like the wrong thing to do. I feel like I'm stealing his things instead of returning them. I put his stuff on the table then I hear someone approaching from the path leading into the trees behind the camper van. I keep reminding myself that I haven't done anything so there's no need to run. Once you've gotten into the habit of going, it's hard to take a break from it.

Anyway, it's him.

He comes along whistling to Bob Marley. He's tall but slightly stooped under the weight of a big, twisty lump of driftwood he's carrying on his back. He's holding a battered paint tin filled with paint-brushes. His navy overalls have their arms wrapped around his waist like they're hugging him. He has a bristly beard on his chin with gray in it, though that could be paint.

Because everything about him is paint.

He has spots and splashes all over his bald head and his face. There are patches on his overalls and on his boots. There's so much on his skin it's like he sweats paint.

His eyes are the color of our bedroom wall.

When he sees me he stops and waves. I walk slowly toward him and as soon as I see his face up close, I'm not scared of him anymore. A small smile sneaks over his face. It makes him look like my dad as if I'd suddenly sprinted twenty years into the future to meet him.

"Do you like Bob Marley?" he asks. I just stand there and nod because I'm having mad thoughts about really traveling into the future and him really being my dad. He holds out his paint splattered hand and says, "Nulty."

"I didn't use your spoon but I washed it anyway," I tell him.

Sometimes I get bored being an idiot all the time.

But it's okay because he just nods like it isn't the stupidest thing he's ever heard in the world ever. He gives me his sneaky grin again so I tell him my name and finally shake his hand. Then we go and sit at the table. He doesn't ask me any questions about what I'm doing here or when I'm leaving. This is a little bit of a letdown because I've invented a sponsored camping trip for charity and I won't get to use it. It took a long time to come up with as well.

Instead, Nulty begins to clean his paintbrushes. I think about offering to help but don't bother when I see how he does it. There's no way I can be that careful about anything. I'm hoping this is because I'm still just a kid so I have a chance to grow out of it. He fills four containers with water from a big blue bucket. He uses the first to work the worst of the paint out of the bristles. He then does the same in the second and then the third container. The final container he uses for a last rinse.

Nulty's fingers are like twists of driftwood with

carefulness and quiet pouring out of them. And just by watching them work I start feeling that way, too—careful and quiet. But not careful in any scared-of-falling kind of way. Nulty doesn't speak while his driftwood fingers work but it doesn't make me want to fill up the quiet they're making. People tell me I normally do that a lot. I'm always filling up quiet spaces with stupid questions[1] or singing or mad noises. I do the last two when I can't think of questions to drive the quiet away. My dad said it's because I'm constantly afraid of quiet because I might have to think something.

But I don't worry about that right now. Nulty's twisty fingers are making the kind of quiet that makes you feel opened out like a flag on a windy day. I do tell him I really liked the curry but I don't tell him it usually makes my bottom explode.

When he's finished with the paintbrushes, Nulty brings water from the stream for us to drink. He pours it into clean jam jars and we then follow the

---

[1] Like, how much poo does someone do in their entire life?

path along the stream and end up on the shore. He's definitely picked the best place on the island to live. There are a lot of trees and rocks to protect his home from the worst storms but it's still bright and open. Nulty takes me down into a little sheltered cove that faces the open sea. There's a small boat sitting upside down to keep the rain out. It's called *The Hope* and is pulled high up the beach out of the reach of the tide. We sit on a massive lump of twisted driftwood that looks like an open hand. We sit on the palm. Near the curly thumb there is a campfire surrounded by a circle of blackened stones. There is also a battered-looking old telescope on a tripod pointing out to sea.

We sit in silence sipping our water for a while. I'm just taking everything in: the sky filled up with daisy-shaped clouds all lying on their sides; the sea smell; the murmur of the waves and the calling seabirds. None of it needs anything to be said about it. Then I notice a black, black ship moving along the distant horizon. It spoils it but part of me is also glad it's there without knowing why. I take off my sneakers and play with the sand between my toes— warm on top and cool underneath. Nulty notices me looking at the ship.

He says, "Try the telescope."

It's a lot more powerful than it looks. The ship takes a big leap toward me. It's an oil tanker. There's a tall bridge at the stern, then it's flat as a paving stone right up to the pointy bit at the front. I notice two people standing side by side looking down over the rail. Suddenly I start to feel sorry for them. It opens up inside me like a big hole. They're just there looking over the side of their big ship and I'm here looking at them through this telescope. The sad feeling is coming from somewhere in between me watching and them not knowing they're being watched. But it's also knowing they wouldn't be able to do anything about it even if they knew.

I stop watching them because it's starting to feel like stealing.

Nulty doesn't say anything but when I sit down again he has this look on his face that says he might know.

We sit watching and not saying much for a while. I get the feeling Nulty's waiting for me to say something but I don't know what it is. Quiet starts pouring out of him again to make me feel quiet again too. I'm glad. Then after a while I need to go before I have to tell him anything. Don't get me wrong—I do want to tell him *something*, I mean, he's been really good to me and all. But I don't want it to come pouring out of me the way it came pouring out Tony Rumsey that time. No. I have to say it all because it's just the right thing to say at just the right time. Besides, I'm busting to ask him about the painting and he hasn't mentioned it for exactly the same reason I have to go, probably.

One hundred and fifty bricks

I don't go straight back to the boathouse; instead I go down to the beach. I've filled up the water bottle again from the stream.[1] For a while I sit on a pile of bricks and try to come up with a reason to stop piling them.

When I finally realize I can't make myself stop and no one else is going to do it for me, I get my hoody from where it's been lying on a rock. It's dried okay but there are thick patches of salt from the water and a big, fat splat of bird poo right in the center of the hood. I must admit I'm impressed by the aim.

My finger and palms become raw and torn again but I keep not stopping.

I really like being filled up to the brim with counting bricks. It must be how my dad feels when

---

[1] Nulty said I could fill it anytime I want.

he's counting things—two always comes after one, no matter what. Just knowing that allows me to feel sure about something. Maybe everyone's counting one, two, three inside themselves all the time. That would be okay. No one would ever have to feel stupid or left out ever again. I asked my dad once and he said he thought it was praying. Then when I didn't know what to say he explained praying is supposed to make you feel better because you're asking to be looked after. I think praying is being scared and admitting you don't know what to do about it. My dad told me counting things made him feel better and also it was asking for something too. When I asked him what it was, he said he didn't know. He said he thought counting things was a strange sort of counting on.

Anyway, I'm so filled up with counting one hundred and fifty bricks I don't notice a big chunk of glass that slices through two of my fingers and makes blood spurt everywhere. I don't really feel it because my hands are sore anyway. I only notice when the bricks I'm carrying feel extra slippery. Then I see the blood dripping off my hoody and staining my jeans. It's so red it doesn't look real. I finish carrying the bricks to the pile, then go down to the shore to wash the cuts. I notice a big rip in my hoody. As soon as I put my hand in the water I realize what a stupid thing it is to do. The saltwater stings like mad and I have a hard time not being sick. I should've used the water bottle instead. When I look down through the water I notice a slice halfway down my little finger and the one right beside it. I snigger a bit because they look like two mouths talking when I move my fingers. They don't hurt apart from the stinging of the water but I know they will. Feeling sick is tied up with not being able to pile any more bricks even though I really, really need to.

When I come out of the water I clench my fist and wrap the hoody around it. My hand feels stretchy and heavy and inflated all at the same time. As I walk back from the shore I can feel all the bricks I've counted come pouring out of me.

At the boathouse I wrap myself up in the paint-spotted sleeping bag and lie there like a rubbish present nobody wants. Thinking this way makes me feel like crying for a bit, so I do. It all comes shuddering out of me because I'm clenched up tight inside myself. It makes me glad to be on my own because one of the things I'm crying about is how Jaffa cakes don't taste as good as they used to. I mean, there's no way I could explain to anyone just how important that is at this second. There just isn't.

I'm glad there are no gulls around at the moment to laugh at me.

The Big Spotty Caterpillar Who Couldn't

When I wake up again it's evening and I can't move my sore hand. There's a dull and distant throbbing that feels like it belongs to someone else. It must've been raining when I was asleep because the sleeping bag is soaking wet and it smells salty and chemically like wee and sweat mixed together. I'm starting to feel very far away as if I'm waving good-bye to myself from the back of a very bumpy bus that has the heating up too high. This makes me laugh a bit but in a mad way. I sit up but stay wrapped up in the sleeping bag like a big, wet spotty caterpillar from a little kid's story called *The Big Spotty Caterpillar Who Couldn't*.

I feel really, really stupid. I know I need some help but I can't get out of the sleeping bag, and the thought of crawling all the way to Nulty's camp makes me feel tired. I think about calling out but that's already turning into wanting to go to sleep and maybe worrying about it tomorrow. My body's like a rubber band that's been stretched too tightly. I just have time to feel stupid about the Jaffa cakes again before I swim away.

Next thing I know is I'm being unwrapped then carried away. But I don't want to go in case Finn comes back. I don't want him to be scared on his own.

The very first thing I notice before I even open my eyes is the deafening sound of rain splattering on a metal roof. The first thing I notice when I open my eyes is a brilliantly colored painted night sky. There are millions of stars and a big fat yellow moon shining down on the sea. The window beside my head has flaking spatters of paint peeling on the glass. I'm warm and not scared anymore and I don't want to move. When I lift up my hand I see a clean bandage wrapped around my cut fingers. I lie for a while counting the painted stars for something to do. I manage two hundred and fifty before the door slides open and Nulty climbs in.

He's wearing the same windcheater from the storm night. I now notice it's covered in different-colored splashes of paint like most things around here. Right now water is dripping from it. Nulty takes it off and puts it to drip dry over a blue basin. He then sits on a chair beside a tiny stove. Neither of us says anything so the silence between us quickly fills up with the sound of drumming rain that wraps itself around everything. I've always liked this sound. It reminds me of holidays. Then behind it or under it I hear the gurgling voice of the little stream. It sounds like someone trying to cure a sore throat.

"There's paint everywhere," I say to Nulty before I realize I've said it. What I really mean is, *What are you painting?*

But Nulty says, "Yes, yes there is."

"Yes," I repeat because all I can think of is how stupid the last thing I said was.

"You cut two of your fingers."

"I was carrying bricks."

"A lot of bricks," he says. As soon as he says it a sneaky sort of smile scoots across his face. It feels like I should explain but I don't say anything because I don't want to yet. Maybe later, but not now.

"Can I see what you're painting?" I ask, and my voice is shaky.

"Tomorrow," Nulty says. He then asks me if I'm hungry and that is the exact moment I realize just how hungry I really am.

I sneak a look over at Nulty as he cooks food on his little stove. It's curry again but I don't care. As I look at him I'm trying to see just what it is that reminds me of my dad. When I finally uncover something like the same shape of nose it just jumbles everything else up and makes him look strange. When he's caught me staring about one million times, Nulty says, "Who is it?"

"Who is it what?"

He grins his sneaky grin.

"I've got one of those faces," he explains.

"What?" I say again. Then once more, "what?"

"One of those faces that always look like someone you know."

"Oh," I reply because I don't want to tell him it's my dad. "Can I still see what you're painting tomorrow even if it keeps raining?"

I stop watching his face and start watching his hands preparing the food. They work in exactly the same slow, quiet way they clean paintbrushes. And as I watch I can imagine those slow, quiet fingers cleaning and bandaging my bloodied fingers like they were paintbrushes or vegetables. Just thinking about these slow, quiet things fills me to the brim. And it doesn't leave any room for that crying, spotty sleeping bag caterpillar who lives in that draughty old boathouse. And there's no room for that vicious, stupid, stuffed otter flattener, either. They make me begin to see again that piling bricks for no reason wasn't a stupid waste of time but as another kind of going and that's that.

Now I suddenly come to know I can eat curry every single night for the rest of my life if waiting for it keeps feeling like this.

"It's curry again," Nulty says. "Is that okay?"

Goldfish

After dinner the rain eases off. Nulty digs out another paint-splattered sleeping bag for me. He also loans me another flashlight which I'm to return tomorrow when I come to see what he's painting. I could have stayed if I had wanted but I couldn't. Sleeping alone in the boathouse is really important because it's a big part of piling bricks.

When I get back I light a small fire just inside the open doorway. It's a bit breezy but there isn't much smoke. I then climb into the sleeping bag and just lay watching the evening[1] and the spluttering little flames and think about things. Not in a bad way or even a mad way, which is unusual for me. No. Thoughts glide slowly in and out of my head like goldfish. It's a really nice slow, quiet feeling I don't need to think about too much. One goldfish

---

[1] The sky is filled with stars and the moon is like a fingernail.

thought is about Finn and me having a wee in the sea with my dad. Inside this goldfish thought, no one is having to count anything because it's just about having a wee in the sea and that's that. This makes another goldfish thought about Angela at the zoo swim along. It's about Angela thinking about two toucans. Whenever she sees something new she has to stop and think about it for a while. And because there were two toucans she made us come back and think about them twice. She saw us laughing and we tried to explain but she didn't get it so we stopped. Another goldfish thought is about me smashing Old Grundy's window but I don't much like that one. But it does make me realize I don't feel guilty about the other fish thoughts. No. I'm just glad I had them in the first place. I hope they can become like slow, quiet fingers. That would be really nice.

BOP

Next day my fingers feel stiff but not as painful. When I come out of the boathouse to have a wee the morning feels strange. It feels like it hasn't decided what to be yet. The trees look like brown and green scribbles. There are clouds in the sky but they're small and separate, like people who don't want anything to do with each other. I'm glad there are no otters again.

When I've finished washing I have the last of a tracker bar and a drink of water. I then go down to the beach. The pile of bricks just lies there doing a good impression of a useless pile of bricks lying on some beach somewhere. I go away quickly because looking at them makes me feel small and useless. I decide to go and see what Nulty has been painting.

I hear more music as I tramp down through the

trees. This time I've no idea who it is. My dad would know because it sounds like jazz and he really likes that sort of thing.

"How's your hand feeling today?" Nulty asks before saying hello or anything. He then changes the bandage and dressing. The cuts now look like the wrinkled mouths of two pensioners in a bus queue having a moan. Thinking about this makes me secret shoulder-shake laugh. This time Nulty bandages them separately. When he's finished he stands up and says, "Follow me."

So I do.

We follow the little path around the camper van to the left. It winds between the trees and every now and then I catch a glimpse of the sea somewhere on my left. I hear it all the time, though, through the music. Somehow it feels really normal walking along this little path behind Nulty and his bobbing bald head. He's taller than I remember but he stoops a lot. I thought it was all the paint tins but he just seems to do it anyway. Maybe he's been doing it for so long his body's just used to stooping. After a couple of minutes of twisting, turning and rising and falling[1] the path curves sharply to the right to go around some rocks. It then stops and opens out into a big glade.

That's when I see it.

It stands about fifty feet high and about the same across. It uses every single bit of space. It's been painted on an old wall standing by itself in the trees. An

---

[1] The island is a lot bigger than I thought.

Otter

I can't believe it. I mean I've come all this way and the last thing I need to see is *this*. It's too mad so I don't say anything.

I wonder why I didn't see it before. I mean, you'd think I would've noticed a fifty-foot otter. Then I remember it is in a big dip and is surrounded by trees.

The rest of the glade is littered with bricks. They must've been part of the building the painted wall belonged to. It also explains my pile of bricks. My beach must be around the headland. We go to a bench made out of driftwood and bricks like the one back at the campsite. We don't say anything for a while because I'm getting over the **Big Otter Painting**. It's nicked everything out of me there is to say, like I'm a sponge it's just squeezed.

Seeing it is jumbling me all up inside. It feels like the otter's been here all along waiting for me. It's standing in almost exactly the same way as Old Grundy's stupid stuffed otter but that's as far as you can compare them. Because this one looks completely alive. Even though it's stuck behind a big pile of scaffolding, it could teach you anything you need to know about being alive. I can see it waiting for night to come; for when the whole world has gone to sleep before finally climbing down then going to the sea.

If I was a BOP, on an old wall, the smell of the sea would drive me mad. I wouldn't be able to wait until nighttime; I'd just climb down and find my giant otter family and maybe stop for a little swim in the sea on the way. But this giant otter wouldn't do that. No. He looks like the most patient giant otter you'd ever meet.

The more I look, the more questions I want to ask. Questions about how and why and for how long? I don't, though, because I'll probably have to answer how and why and for how long as well. So I stay quiet and stare at the BOP staring back at me. After a while its big brown eyes start burrowing through me. Then the crisscross scaffolding makes it look like a zoo or a giant otter prison. In fact it looks a bit sad.

"Do you think he looks sad?" Nulty asks. I'm now a bit spooked in case he knows what I'm thinking. So I just nod slowly for a bit. A nod can mean anything if you want it to.

I nod for a bit longer then I forget and ask: "How long have you been painting this big otter for?"

"Ten years," he says.

"I'm ten," I point out.

"That's a long, long time, isn't it?"

I try nodding again while I think of a good question to ask him.

"Do you want to know why?" he asks, reading my mind again. When I sneak a look at his face I'm just in time to see his sneaky grin scoot across him again. Nulty stands up then hands me a paintbrush.

This is how I start to help.

And it feels right.

If you'd told me on Monday I'd be helping to paint a giant otter on a big wall now I would have thought you'd lost your marbles. It just goes to show you.

Here goes . . .

Nulty hasn't said a word since he handed me his long letter and told me it's about what happened to him and his family. He looks at me then, smiles and tells me I don't have to read it right now. I'm really glad because I hate people staring at me when I'm doing anything. I also know it's supposed to be my turn and I don't know why I need to hold on to it but I do. That's a lie—I do know.

I'm scared stiff.

Anyway, I can't put it off anymore, so here goes. . . .

What Nulty Wrote . . .

◎

I lived a normal life for a very long time, as normal as any. I was an art teacher; I had a wife and a son. I loved them. Then I lost them in a boating accident. After the funeral I found I couldn't be around people anymore. I was overcome with the feeling that I knew something they didn't. And that sets you apart. I looked at people and saw them so filled up with their lives and their survival they could only remind me of how empty I was.

I began to stay inside, to hide from people. It was a kind of running away without really going anywhere. I took to only coming out at night. When I needed food I went to shops far from where I lived. I wanted to avoid those who knew me. I felt accused by their looks of concern and their words of sympathy. I thought I was responsible for the death of my family even though I knew I couldn't be. I had survived them when all I wanted to do was to be lost with them. I was angry that they had left me behind. Breathing became a punishment, a strange kind of judgement.

After a time I went into hospital. When I came out I took early retirement. The guilt and the anger had gone but in their place was a strange sort of emptiness that ached like a wound. You know how it is, when you're scared of something, you want to escape it. So I decided to try and outrun the emptiness. I sold our house and bought a camper van. There was insurance money from the accident but I couldn't make myself touch it. I gave it away and immediately felt lighter. It didn't make the emptiness go away but things seemed a bit better.

Then I began to drive.

On the first day I left my complete book collection by the side of the road for whoever wanted it. Then bit by bit I gave everything away that had belonged to my life with my family. I have no idea why I would give a particular thing away to one person rather than another. But what I did know was that the emptier the van became, the lighter I felt, and the clearer things began to seem. Finally there was just one thing left; a photograph of us together. That was the only thing I couldn't give away.

As I drove, the world gradually began to mean something to me again: a place to be driven through. So that's what I did, I drove and drove and drove. I only stopped to eat, sleep, buy petrol or repair the van.

After traveling for a long time I found this island and drove across at low tide. I decided to rest for a week, and even though I had stopped my mind was still moving, the way a record keeps turning even after you've switched it off. Then I realized the driving had been beyond my control, like running downhill and not being able to stop. I parked just up from the boathouse. But I couldn't bring myself to leave the van. The outside world was too big, too much for me.

I began to watch a family of otters who lived near the beach. After a few days I opened the van door and began to draw them on the inside of food wrappers and scraps of paper. They were quite tame. They completely ignored me. Finally I stepped outside into the most beautiful moonlit night I have ever seen.

After that I spent all my time drawing and photographing the otter family. Then one morning I woke up to find them gone. A terrible panic seized me because I'd forgotten the emptiness and now it was threatening to return.

So I began to explore. The first thing I noticed there were bricks lying everywhere. I followed their trail.

That was how I found the wall.

It had been part of a building destroyed by a storm. It was completely covered in creepers and ivy. But looking at it made something move inside me. The wall felt like a presence that had been waiting here for me all along.

That's when I decided to stay.

I had no idea why I was doing this. It was one of those times that you have to just trust your feelings and see what happens. All I had to go on was the certainty that I needed to paint something big. This came as a shock to me. You see I hadn't wanted to paint anything for a long time. In fact my painting equipment was part of what I'd given away.

Then one morning I was sitting by the shore watching the tide turning when I saw them.

A family of otters were hunting for fish about fifty yards offshore. That's when I knew exactly what I needed to paint.

I drove about fifty miles and filled the van with all the supplies I needed. The scaffolding was the most difficult. It took four trips and I was worried about the camper van not being able to make it.

The next day I went straight to the wall and worked until it was too dark to see. I took my sleeping bag from the van and slept by the wall. As soon as it was light I began to work again. And that was how things were for two weeks.

A new rhythm had begun.

I built the scaffolding in the evening and painted during the day. I used what light there was to paint. Sometimes I just slept where I fell. Sometimes I'd wake up covered in insect bites. One morning I found that a spider had spun its web between my ear and a paint tin. At first I didn't dream, then I dreamed of the otter for six nights in a row. The only time I left the wall was to buy more materials or food. I was living on apples and sweet-and-sour pot noodles. When the weather was too bad to work on the otter, I painted the ceiling of the camper van instead. A starry sky seemed the right thing to do. I was too scared to stop painting in case I couldn't start again.

One morning on the high scaffolding I began to cry because I had no red paint left. I continued painting but cried for two days until I felt so light I could have walked on air.

Everything I know about the world is poured into that otter painting. I can feel it in the texture of the paint and the roughness of the old bricks underneath. Each and every thing I know about myself has turned into this: being a boy, then becoming a man, that man becoming a husband and then a father and then a man again, a man who has lost everything; a man who has to paint this giant otter on this old, abandoned wall to explain all his loss to himself.

Then during a storm part of the head was damaged enough for me to have to repaint it. And when I finished the repair something made me keep going. Now each time I come close to finishing I have to start from the beginning again. Each time I put on a new layer the otter seems more substantial, more capable of existing by itself. It's as if the explanation I need isn't in the painting but buried somewhere deep inside the act of painting it.

I've come to realize there isn't any reason for what has happened to my life. And although I know it I can't seem to make myself stop looking for it here in this paint and deep inside these old bricks beneath it. I know I can only be released from this wall if it's washed away by another great storm like the one that created it.

Nulty

Gull Toilet

I go back to the boathouse to sleep. The pile of bricks
I've built is bigger than I remember. But it still looks
really lonely and abandoned lying there on the sand.
Some gulls are standing on it, practicing laughing at
me. But I don't care about that. Looking at that big,
lonely gull toilet of bricks gives me a sort of sick feeling deep in my belly. It's that sick feeling you get
when you know something is about to change.

I light my fire. As I build it I notice my hands are
still covered in paint spots. There's even paint on the
bandages. Then I look at my clothes and they're
covered too. For some reason all this paint bothers me
enough to go and wash a bit in the sea. When I'm
cleaning my stinging hands, I think about some of the
things I told Nulty. It poured out of me after all.

Nulty didn't say a word.

What I said to Nulty

My family is my mum and my dad and my identical twin brother and my little sister, Angela, who's deaf, and Donut the thick dog. We lived together in this house on Holt Street. My brother was drowned. It happened at a river a few miles from our house. This is what happened. . . .

Finn always loved otters since the time we went to the otter sanctuary when we were six. He loved them so much he got our Irish nan to knit him a brown sweater with an otter on the front. He did it by mentioning it every time he spoke to her on the phone so she wouldn't forget. He got me to mention it all the time too. My dad fixed us up to a live webcam about otters who lived in America somewhere. Anyway there's a weir on the river near our house. And otters are mad about weirs. There was an article about a family of otters with two young cubs in our local newspaper. They are making a comeback in our bit of the world. Finn cut out a picture of the weir and put it on the wall above our bunk bed. We're usually not allowed to do that because Blu Tack leaves an oily stain.

After that Finn started hounding my dad to take us to see that otter family. When he was bored doing it he asked me to take over because he said no one can tell us apart. Dad gave his odd laugh then finally gave in but we'd have to wait until half term. My dad was very busy with exams at the time. Finn and me knew the cubs would be grown and gone by then. So I came up with a plan to sneak out late one Friday night. We were going through the whole commando thing at the time. We'd been bought camouflage pajamas by our mad aunt. People were always buying us matching stuff for some reason. The plan was to sneak out, then cycle to the river on our matching BMX bikes we'd gotten for Christmas.

We picked the night, then got our commando stuff ready. We packed our walkie-talkies so we could split up and watch from different places. We even practiced sneaking up and down stairs to find the creaks in the floorboards. It was a really good laugh. So that Friday night Finn and me snuck out like commandoes or something. Finn had hidden our bikes in the front hedge so we wouldn't have to go near the garage.

We didn't turn on our lights until we were about a mile away from the house. It had been raining all day but the clouds had cleared for us and a big fat moon had come out. It was really good weather for spotting otters. We were both really excited. We heard the river before we saw it. Then we could smell it, too. We hid our bikes away. Then we crept along toward the weir. The water was flowing fast and the river was big and swollen with all the rain. That was the only sound and movement. Everything else was shadowy and still and a bit spooky. Neither of us had ever been out on our own so late before. I noticed I was shaking a bit. I couldn't tell if Finn was. Then we crept down the bank.

The water on the weir was black and smooth but you could tell by the ripples it was swirling underneath. There was a little narrow plank bridge running to the other side. It had one little hand bar to hold on to. The bridge was painted white like bones and stood out very clearly in the moonlight.

We played Rock, Paper, Scissors to see who would go across to the other side, because there was a better spot over there. Finn won. He scooted across the bridge to the other side. Then he vanished into the opposite darkness. I crouched down and watched the river for about twenty minutes, then my walkie-talkie crackled. It was Finn asking if I'd seen anything. He hadn't and I told him I hadn't, either. I radioed him about thirty minutes after that because I was bored and freezing. I just wanted to go home. We agreed to give it another ten minutes or so. Then Finn radioed me again and said he was coming back. About a second later he radioed again. He seemed to be whispering so I held the walkie-talkie close to my ear. Finn did this deafening fart into the radio. It was so loud I could almost smell it. Then he was sniggering like a monkey.

It was the last sound I ever heard him make.

A couple of seconds later he appeared on the little footbridge. He was a dark, moving boy-shape against the whiteness of the bridge. He waved over to me and I waved back.

Then he was gone.

At first I didn't realize what had happened. When I did I still couldn't believe it. I thought about what I was going to tell our mum and dad. As I ran on to the bridge everything became really cold and started to slow down. Then the whole world became exactly like somewhere I'd never been before. I had to stop and think for a moment for the wooden thing I was standing on to become a bridge.

There was no sign of him and I was left alone with the roar and the smell of the river.

They found me downriver from the weir. I was soaking wet and covered in mud. I'd been looking for him all night. They had to work out what had happened because I'd forgotten how to speak words. I just sat in the mud on the bank trembling. I didn't speak for a long time after that. My dad said it was six weeks. I couldn't make myself say my name. He was counting by then. I thought if they couldn't tell who I was, they couldn't tell who was lost either. I was really glad because it meant that he was still here.

Nothing was the same in our house. It looked the same but that just made missing it feel worse. Dad was even counting in his sleep and mum was wondering what a real mother looked like. Angela just kept on trying to hug everyone all the time. I think she knew who I was. But no one would say anything. I reminded them of him every single second. We became like a bunch of rubbish actors acting in a rubbish film about us pretending to be normal. All except Angela who just kept on being her real, true self. She doesn't know how to be a rubbish actor yet. Donut just spent the time whining by the kitchen door as if he wanted to look for him. While I was trying to be invisible by guessing where mum and dad wouldn't be, I began to find Dad's long counting things lists all over the place. Then I began to find my mum's little notes to herself as well. They were hidden in millions of different places. But when you're a kid no one can hide stuff in your house without you knowing. She started worrying about every little mum thing she did. She was always phoning Nan every two seconds because she didn't trust anything about herself anymore. That's when she started forgetting things. One time someone found her parked by the side of the road trying to remember where we lived.

After that I put the three-holed brick through Old Grundy's window and flattened his stupid stuffed otter. And I'm not sorry I did it. Not one tiny, little bit. I'm sorry it had to be Old Grundy's window. But I would still do it again right this second if I got the chance. I wouldn't even have to think about it. Finn hated that stuffed otter and he was scared of it. He had dreams about it coming to get him. He said it was because it was made to look alive but they had to kill it first.

Having a laugh

I'm so angry with him for leaving us, for leaving me behind. How could he have been so stupid as to slip off that stupid bridge? How could he do that? I really wish I had him here for just ten seconds so I could kick his head in. Because of him I don't know who to be anymore. I don't know anything. I'm only a kid; I'm not supposed to be thinking these things or saying these things or feeling these things. I'm supposed to be having a laugh and maybe learning a bit along the way.

You probably think I'm some sort of evil creature that you definitely don't want to have helping you paint your big otter painting you can't finish. In fact you probably want to boot me off the island altogether. I wouldn't blame you if you did.

I know my mum and dad and little sister are

worried about where I am. I know hurting them this way is a terrible thing to do. But it was hurting more having me there. I could see it. I just had to go. I couldn't stand seeing them forget for a second, then remembering as soon as they saw me over and over and over again. I can't stand them blaming themselves. It was me. It was my fault. It was always my fault. I'd give anything to *be* him right now. Even if it meant they had to forget about me forever. It would be worth it.

All I know about for sure is just how easy it is for the people you worry about to disappear or get flattened.

If there is a god somewhere, I don't think he likes us very much. But I don't want there to be one. I want it all to happen by accident. It makes it a lot easier to bear slides flattening people if no one is pushing them over.

My dad thinks God has gone on a permanent break. I don't know if that's true. Before what happened, I used to think it was just stuff. I mean the most interesting thing I could find to think about God was his name spelt backward is dog. Since then I've found myself thinking about him more. My mum thinks that people invented God to help themselves cope better and to help explain bad things when they happen. If that's true, then I don't think it's worked very well. The only kind of god I can think of that would be any use having is one who dashes about saving people from being flattened— a bit like Spider-Man only better. If he does the opposite, such as pushing slides on top of people, then it would be much better if he was on a permanent break. The only thing I know for sure is if he is sitting up in heaven or wherever and just watching then he needs a thump. Sitting and watching it happen and not doing anything about it is almost exactly as bad as making it happen in the first place.

Poo spots

When I wake up next day I do the normal morning things. But I do them in an emptied out kind of way. As if saying all that I said has used me up for a while. I don't go near the half-finished pile of bricks. I don't want them to make me feel small and drab and pointless, which I am now very bored of feeling. Just for a little while it would be nice to feel big and bright and whatever the opposite to pointless is. So I don't even look in the general direction of that pile of bricks, that seagull toilet. But I also know there's just it and me on the whole of this beach together and we can't get away from each other.

Next thing I know my feet are taking me toward it.

I stare at it for a while and play Join the Poo Spots in my head. Then I notice something: I'm not feeling small and drab and pointless; I'm playing

Join the Poo Spots instead. As soon as I know this, I know something massive and scary. I know I'm here to pile bricks until I've piled enough. I'm not here to keep Nulty company painting a giant otter painting that can't ever be finished. I'm a brick piler and I have to explain that to Nulty face-to-face. Definitely a PBTM. I mean, after all we've said to each other, then I go and refuse to help him paint his big otter.

Anyway I go straight to Nulty's camp before I have a chance to think about it. It seems to take a lot longer to get there than before. It's as if the camp has been moved twenty miles in the night and my feet have been replaced with lead weights. There isn't any music so all I can hear is my feet clump-clumping as I stumble stupidly around in the trees. I've noticed things tend to go like this when you're scared of doing something. Things get far away and moved around; time speeds up or slows down, depending on what mood it is in.

When I get to the camp, there's no sign of him. I think about going to the big otter painting but I don't want to see it again. It feels like it's none of my business anymore. So I sit for a while instead. Then I notice a pair of heavy work gloves lying on the table. They have this note attached to them:

Useful for piling bricks.
P.S. Come to dinner tonight.

Three thousand bricks

Even with the work gloves my hand still hurts. But I manage to push it outside counting bricks. I think: *Okay, pain in my fingers, I'm going to put you down here and think about you later.* By lunchtime I've managed to add ninety-six new bricks to the pile. It's getting harder because I have to go farther around the headland to find new bricks to pile and I'm getting nearer to the BOP. Then it starts to rain, so I run back to the boathouse and spend the time reading my best bits from *Huckleberry Finn*. Then the rain clears away by mid afternoon and I manage to add another forty-seven bricks by dinnertime.

I've decided to stop piling when I reach three thousand bricks. If I don't know by then, then I doubt if I ever will. Knowing this makes me feel more sure and solid inside.

Bye-bye

There is that flat splattering of rain on the tin roof overhead that always sounds like it's about to fill everything up. The sliding door is half open to let out the cooking steam. Through it the rain is a gray transparent curtain that lets you know what it would feel like behind a waterfall. There is the smell of curry in the air. It all looks the same but feels completely different.

We definitely don't talk about piling bricks or painting giant otters. No. It feels like we've come through all that, through all the talking to this. Only I don't know what *this* is. Still, it could be worse. It could be sweet-and-sour pot noodle for dinner.

When we've finished eating and I've done the washing up, we sit by the half-open door and Nulty changes the dressing on my fingers. I'm watching the rain making sizzling little jumps from puddle to puddle and back again the way Angela does exactly one million miles away. This doesn't make me feel sad. I'm actually enjoying it.

"Would it be okay to see the photograph of your family?" I ask because it seems okay to do so. Without looking up or speaking, Nulty reaches inside a drawer for the photograph then passes it to me. It's battered and wrinkled a bit. I'm surprised when I see his son. For some reason I thought of him as being ten like me. But he looks much older, at least seventeen. He looks like his mum but he has the same sneaky grin as his dad. His mum looks happy and worried at the same time the same way my mum does sometimes.

"Do you know what worries me the most?" Nulty asks without looking up from my hand.

"No. What?"

"What he would look like in all the other moments in his life."

I don't know what Nulty means so I don't speak. I'm hoping it will get simpler as it goes along.

"His face in that photograph is waiting to look like him when he's thirty or when he becomes someone's dad for the first time. Only it'll never happen now. He's trapped there as that version of himself forever. It feels as if he's becoming reduced to just that photograph, no before, no after. I'm scared I'm forgetting him."

I don't really understand any of this but it feels like I should or will later.

"Do you think your mum and dad feel this way?" he suddenly asks me.

"Dunno," I tell him, but as soon as I say it I know that I do know. His question pushes some kind of button deep inside me. Nothing happens but I know something big has changed. I also know that when something happens inside me I'm usually the last to know.

After that I go back to the boathouse.

2029

As soon as the sun wakes me up I start piling bricks again. And although I'm quickly filled up with counting bricks, I keep thinking about the last thing Nulty said to me about his son. Imagine having to lose someone twice like that. I mean to feel them slowly being vacuumed out of your memory like bread crumbs down the back of the settee until it felt you'd dreamed them up in the first place. No wonder he needs to keep painting and painting and painting that big otter of his. Maybe doing it isn't like being in prison at all and I'm just being really thick the way I normally am. I mean, he doesn't act like someone who's in prison. He said doing it and continuing to do it was the only way he could make sense to himself. So maybe it's not a question of him keeping everything that makes sense inside himself but keeping everything outside that doesn't make sense to him. Even though this sounds really stupid, it feels right.

Maybe that's why when I try to think of brick piling and otter painting as the same thing, I can't manage it. The difference is I want to finish piling bricks. I want to be able to say, *Okay that's finished, now. . . .*

I don't want to keep everything out.

As soon as I think through all this I know something new. This is it: *I'm almost finished.* These words come splashing through me like skimming stones. They make me shiver but not in a scared way. No. Even though I'm holding a stack of bricks, they feel as light as a bubble.

I spend the rest of the day piling bricks like mad.

By lunchtime I'm beginning to wonder what the last brick will look like. I think:

Will it look different?

Will it feel heavier?

Will it feel lighter?

Will it have three holes?

I think about the last brick until I'm bored stupid. Then I start worrying about what will happen if I get so bored looking for it I miss it. I mean, what if I've only got one go at finding it? And if I miss this one last sneaky brick, will I have to go on piling bricks forever?

I get so lost inside all this mad thinking I don't even notice it's raining until I'm soaked through and shivering. I don't stop piling bricks.

And then I've found it.

It happens like this. I just reach down and pick up a third brick to add to the pile and just know that's it. Don't ask me how I know I just do. And:

It doesn't look any different

It doesn't feel any heavier

It doesn't feel any lighter

It does have three holes.

I hold it in my hand and watch the big fat

raindrops go splat-splat-splat on it: brick number 2029.

I stand for ages thinking about what I have to do with the bricks. Because now I've finished piling them, I do know. It was like it was waiting for me to finish all along. I don't know why I know it, I just do, and it's a very certain kind of knowing.

Then I just start.

Finished

I finish it by lunchtime.

Then I go and collect all the things Nulty loaned me. I know what I need to do now. It's so obvious I almost feel a bit stupid. But that kind of thinking doesn't seem to stick to me anymore. And I feel bigger.

When I reach his camp there's no sign of the van. Nulty has gone; and the place looks completely wrong without him. Everything else is where it should be. The shelter, the driftwood table, the chairs, the potted plants, everything. But it seems out of balance. I think about waiting even though I can't stay. Now that I know where to go and what I need to do when I get there, I'm restless to do it. I place the sleeping bag and the water bottles and the flashlight on the driftwood table. I then spend about an hour writing "thank you" in millions of small, white stones. I do it right beside the table so he won't miss it.

Then I leave.

It feels like one million years have passed since the night of the storm. I must admit I feel a bit sorry for that little scared me back then. But I don't feel scared now, not right this second—and I think that must be the most you can hope for.

I have one last wee in the sea, then cross with squelchy feet to the mainland. I stop about halfway up the hill toward the train station for a rest. The clouds have all cleared away except for one massive one that looks like my dad doing an impression of a potato.[1] This is a bit mad but I don't mind.

I know you'll never be able to see the words from outer space. But looking back down at them from right here is okay by me. And I didn't even spell it wrong. It says:

---

[1] He can't help doing this impression.

Finn
Was
Here

Part Three

Being

One million feelings

I hear the river before I see it and I smell it just before that. It sounds angry, as if it's in no mood to be reminded of anything. But I don't care. As I come closer it begins to roar, then I see it gleaming through the trees. Everything about it—sight and sound and smell—comes sneaking up to surround me. But I don't care about that, either. No. I need to do what I've come here to do. I feel a wave of hatred for this river come pouring through me. I hate it because it's completely flattened everything. It's reached in and jumbled up my family like Lego bricks. But I've stopped wanting to block it off or fill it in or pollute it with nuclear waste. It can't seem to help itself anymore than a giant slide can help being a giant slide.

I pass along the bank toward the weir. I can feel

myself beginning to shiver. Now I can see that terrible little plank bridge, the one that's painted white, the one that looks like bones. There's about one million feelings colliding inside me. Most of them are shouting at me to run away. But I won't. Because there's something else that's shouting louder. This is where I need to be right now.

Nobody's fault

Now I'm really, really scared. I can feel my heart beating like mad and my mouth is filling up with spit. I feel a bit like being sick but it's a sort of distant feeling. I also need a poo. But none of these things will make me leave. I know if I let being scared take charge of me right now I'll never get out from under it ever, ever again. Also if I run I'll be letting him down. And I don't ever want to do that again, no matter what. And now I know something else too. And here it is: *It wasn't my fault.* I also know my family would have felt the exact same way if it had been me instead of him. And it wouldn't have been his fault, either. My mum would still be worrying about what a mum is; my dad would still be counting things like mad; and Angela would still be hugging anyone she could get her hands on. And they weren't doing it because of me. No. They were doing it because they are people and that's the sort of thing people do when they lose someone.

People are stuck with having to worry about things flattening those they worry about. They also have to deal with it when it finally happens. It's easy to believe it won't happen because it can keep on not happening for a long time. I think that must be why people are rubbish at dealing with it when someone does finally get flattened out of the blue. It's because everything we think we know about the world gets flattened, too. And even people who aren't part of your family get shaken by it. Because you remind them that all they tricked themselves into believing is just that—a trick. That's why Airplane Kev acted like it was something he could catch off me. And it isn't just him either. People treat you like a bad smell even as they're trying like mad not to.

I really want to blame this river for taking my brother away from me and wrecking my family. But there isn't much point. I mean, you may as well blame rain for being wet. So I'm stuck. The only thing I can think of doing is to try and forget blaming anyone for anything. I don't know if I'll be able to but I know I'll have to try.

Photograph

It's not a bad thing to look exactly like my brother.

When he is eleven and twelve and twenty; when he is happy and when he is sad; when he feels lonely or when he is glad to be with someone; when he wins something and when he loses it; when he cuts his knee and when he tries to save Angela from the big slide. To see him doing these things I only need to sneak a peek in a puddle or a shop window or in someone's eyes and there he'll be: living and laughing and crying and not being forgotten.

I can't really imagine myself doing any of these things. I'm stuck inside its terrible sight and sound and smell. But I also know I won't always be.

Even though I'm scared stiff now and will probably go on being scared stiff for ages I won't let it beat me. And that's not because I'm being brave or any rubbish like that. No. It is because there doesn't seem to be any other choice.

Don't ask me why I suddenly know all this stuff because I haven't a clue. And I don't know what most of it means. I hope to work it out as I go along, because that's all you can do.

Weeing again

I put my right foot on the little plank bridge. For a
second I look down past it and watch the black
water pouring over the edge of the weir. I hold on
to the handrail then walk slowly out to the middle
of the bridge. I stop there and stare down into the
swirling water below. I am shaking all over. I am
suddenly really scared of tumbling into that black,
vicious water. And the feeling is so strong I stop
breathing for a second. I'm trying very hard not to
imagine how cold that water must feel. Then I'm
breathing again and I'm not shaking as much. I do
a wee down into the water. And it seems to last forever. When I'm finished I stop for a second and
watch the steam vanish, then I turn and come to the
bank.

Now I have to go back home. Now I know I

have to stop pretending and be myself. I have to stop pretending. I know I've caused my family a lot of pain but even now I can't think of any other way I could have got past what happened. I'm sorry, but only that it all had to happen in the first place. I had to *go* because when I finally spoke after those stupid six weeks they found out I was *me* and not my brother.

He's gone for good.

Before I go home I stop for one last look at the river. This is when I see a sudden movement out of the corner of my eye. It's immediately followed by a splash of something chasing something else. It was too quick for me to see but it feels bigger than a water rat. I wait for a second but there isn't anything else. I turn and walk toward the road. This is when I see him. He must have been there the whole time. He says, "Hello Finn."

And I think, *Yes, yes that's me.* So I say, "Hello, Dad."

Then we walk home together.